Saint's Ride

THE SAINTS OF LAREDO

BOOK ONE

GRACE DONOVAN

Phase Publishing, LLC
Seattle

Text copyright © 2017 by Phase Publishing, LLC
Cover art copyright © 2017 by Phase Publishing, LLC

Cover design by Christopher Bailey

Phase Publishing, LLC first paperback edition
May 2017

ISBN 978-1-943048-28-1
Library of Congress Control Number: 2017940524
Cataloging-in-Publication Data on file.

Acknowledgments

This book is dedicated to my amazing family and friends, supportive through all things, thick and thin, and most especially to my friend and fellow romance writer, Rebecca Connolly. Without your encouragement of a crazy idea and some great soundtrack suggestions, this never would have happened.

And to my love. More than a Saint, you're an Angel.

 Prologue

FALLS CITY, NEBRASKA

1880

Jack idly swirled the whiskey in his glass. His eyes were trained on the rich, golden liquid, but his attention was on the ladies at the edges of his vision.

The women were all employees of the establishment that Jack now sat in, back in a corner with the brim of his hat pulled low. The place was a saloon by name, but everyone knew more than just drinking went on here. Not that it would have been hard to guess as much, considering the manner of dress the gals were sporting.

Low-cut, brightly-colored corsets, heavily frilled skirts with the sides pinned up to show the tops of the girls' garters, even the ribbons in their hair were designed to draw attention, and then only to redirect it further down to more interesting areas.

Plain as can be, most of the women likely got a great deal more attractive to potential customers the more of the surprisingly good whiskey they drank, but despite his third glass, Jack hadn't even started to feel tipsy yet. The Hannity men had always held their liquor well. Besides, Jack wasn't here for that kind of business.

He had a contract, and though it did involve a woman here, it didn't have a thing to do with sex, and nothing to do with the ladies already here. Jack hadn't yet seen the woman he was looking for, but knew she'd be along soon enough.

Word was she was quite the fiery woman, which didn't bother Jack in the least. He'd brought in criminals much bigger, stronger, and meaner than any woman could ever be. This gal wouldn't be a problem.

Jack had just raised the glass to his lips when the doors opened in the back of the room, and she walked in. He knew it was her the instant he laid eyes on her. Only years of hard living gave him the self-control to keep his composure as he forced down the swallow of smooth whiskey.

He'd gotten detailed descriptions of Evelyn Delano from both her father and a few other folks there in town Jack had spoken to while tracking her here. Everything they'd told him was true and accurate, but it still didn't come close to describing the woman who walked through those doors as if she owned the place. Which, in fact, she did. She was fiercely stunning, in the same sense that a tornado was beautiful.

Jack knew immediately that this woman was going to be trouble.

Her dark hair curled everywhere, despite being pulled back in an elegant manner, but the expression on her face made it look more like a nest of angry vipers than the delicate style she'd obviously been aiming for. It also made her striking blue eyes look cold as ice.

Jack was half-surprised she wasn't carrying her own private storm cloud over her head, lightning lancing every which way. As those piercing eyes cast around the room, Jack turned quickly away so she wouldn't realize he'd been watching her. He'd actually forgotten to stick to his peripheral vision and mentally cursed himself. He couldn't help but look back at her, though, as her furious expression reflected in the cutting tones of her angry voice when she spotted her quarry.

"Parsons! If I've told you once, I as sure as the day is long won't tell you twice," she snapped.

Jack noted with interest that she wasn't moving toward the man she glared at, but rather was walking with a fiercely graceful determination behind the bar. The gals Jack had been watching earlier had all moved quickly to the sides of the room, far away from the man she addressed with such venom.

The man in question, Parsons, Jack assumed, was scrambling away from the uncomfortable-looking girl whose arm he'd been tightly gripping. Even from here, Jack could see the bruising starting to form where his hand had been. The woman he'd been gripping looked frightened, but not of Evelyn Delano.

"I told you, Parsons, if I ever saw your face around my place again, I'd fill you full of buckshot!" Sure enough, her slender arms came up from behind the bar with a sturdy, well-maintained shotgun.

"Miss Delano!" a man in wire-framed spectacles down the bar called in alarm, but it was too late. Evelyn Delano pulled the trigger.

People, men and women alike, screamed and dove to the ground as her blast, which missed by a fair margin despite her mark not having moved a lick out of sheer shock and terror, blew a sizeable chunk out of two of the wall boards.

Jack had rolled out of his chair and to the floor the moment he'd seen the shotgun coming up, and he already had his Colt in hand, hammer back and ready. Not because of the shotgun, which wasn't pointed even remotely his direction, but just in case Parsons had drawn his own gun to shoot back. Jack needed Miss Delano alive and unharmed, or the contract was void. He needn't have worried. Parsons still didn't move, until she aimed to fire again.

The man bolted like a scared rabbit. Jack whistled low in awe as the shotgun fired a second time, the buckshot shattering another board just over Jack's table as Parsons scrambled for the door, shards of wood shrapnel stinging his cheek.

Jack looked back at Evelyn Delano in amazement. She had already broken open the shotgun and emptied the spent shells, deftly catching two more from the big barkeep, who tossed them almost casually, with an amused expression on his face.

Parsons made it out the door just as Evelyn locked the barrels back into place and readied the shotgun for a third shot. Lowering the gun angrily as her quarry escaped, she spat a very un-ladylike word.

Jack eased the hammer back down on his Colt and holstered it as he righted his upended chair and slid back into it. Picking a couple shards of wood from his whiskey glass, he downed the rest in a quick gulp. Fiery wasn't the right word for this woman, Jack decided as she handed the shotgun back to the bartender, who took it and replaced it beneath the bar without a word. The woman was an absolute spitfire. For a moment, he wondered if this one would be worth the bounty.

"Sorry about that, folks," she said, tucking a now-errant strand of curly hair back behind her ear. "Just a bit of a fuss with a former customer. Can't have anyone manhandling my ladies, am I right?" she asked with a smile. There were a number of muttered and half-hearted agreements as all the men in the room watched the woman cautiously, as if she was an angry mountain lion. "Next round is on me, boys. Girls, get to making these fine gentleman feeling welcome." The response to her last two statements was much more enthusiastic.

Jack shook his head slightly as the bartender began taking orders for that free round of drinks. This changed things, he knew. He'd need to be stone sober to handle this wildcat. Talking would get him nowhere with this one. His steel gray eyes fixed on Evelyn Delano, his mind working as he came up with a new plan. He leaned back and considered.

Miss Delano made a circuit of the room, stopping to talk to any of the patrons who still looked a bit uneasy. Her features had changed dramatically as she'd lost the furious glower. Her soft smile and easy demeanor put people at their ease, just as quickly as her wrath had set them on edge. Jack was fascinated, despite himself.

Her features were pretty, though that wasn't what had caught his attention. Not entirely, at any rate. Every move, every smile, every word, seemed to be filled with an energy he'd never seen before. After a while, he realized he'd stopped planning, and had just been thinking about her. Not good, Jack, he told himself. Stay on the job and keep sharp. Losing focus was how a man got killed in his line of work.

Another few minutes, and he had his plan in mind. Standing smoothly, he quietly set a quarter on the table for his drinks, then turned and walked out the door.

Chapter One

Evie sighed as she closed the door to her private room above the saloon. She knew she'd lose customers over this, but she also knew it was right. Her girls were there by choice, and every one had been given other options, either by their own families or by Evie herself. She had no indentured girls, no girls who felt trapped, or that this was their only life choice. All six had chosen this life, free and clear. Except herself, of course.

She would not stand by and let any of her girls be hurt by abusive customers. She shouldn't have shot at him, she knew. The threat of the gun in her hands alone would have been more than enough to send that simpering coward running away like his hair was on fire.

Evie knew better, though. It might have been enough to keep him away, but it might not have been enough for the next man who thought he could do whatever he liked to her girls. This way, he'd talk about the crazy shrew who'd shot at him. She'd lose some potential customers that way, but most of the men she lost would be types like Parsons, the rotten dog.

Of course, the cost of repairing the two walls, and a room full of free drinks wasn't going to do wonderful things for her cash supply, either. All of that said, it sure was fun, and more than a little satisfying, she thought.

Sighing again, she moved to the small desk by the window. She could afford the repairs, if only just. Her girls were well paid, and Evie kept enough to keep the place running and to save a few dollars for eventual retirement, but nothing more. It was worth it, she knew. Her girls needed to feel safe, and her crazy antics were sure to reassure the girls that she'd do absolutely anything to protect them.

Picking up her ledger, she began looking over the numbers, but she couldn't really focus on them. Which was probably a good thing.

Evie was glad she hadn't hit the man, though she doubted she could have if she'd tried. She was grateful for Ben, her bartender and bouncer, for teaching her how to release the barrel for reloading, or she'd have looked like a complete fool.

It was literally the second time she'd ever held a shotgun, the first being when Ben had given her the lesson. In case of emergencies, she'd told him, but she never thought she'd actually need to use the thing.

In any case, she said to herself, nobody had been hurt, she'd protected her girls, reassured them that she would fight to keep them safe, and had furthered her reputation as a dangerous, crazy person. All of that was good, except for her own reputation. It wasn't as if available men were lining up to vie for her hand, even before this latest incident.

She had long ago given up on finding a husband for herself. Not since the fiasco with Frank, anyway. Still, a part of her wanted what most women wanted; a comfortable life, with a husband she adored, who loved her dearly and respected her strength and intelligence, and a couple of children running around the house. Setting down the ledger, she rubbed the bridge of her nose between two fingers.

Not going to happen, Evie, she told herself. She knew better than to get caught in that mental trap. That nonsense was precisely what had brought her to run away with Frank from her home in Topeka. It was either that or let her father marry her off for a political favor. Prostitution was one thing though she'd never actually done that herself, but someone else selling her virtue and life away for their own gain? It was outright slavery, and she would have none of that!

In the end, Frank was gone, her father was a horrible person she never wanted to see again, and all she had was this place and her girls. It was a far cry better than many unmarried women had it these days, she knew. Somehow, that didn't stop her from occasionally letting her mind wander on what might have been. If Frank hadn't turned out to be such a mangy curr, that is. Now him, she should have shot.

A knock at the door caused her to turn in her chair.

"Come on in," she said. The door opened, and Ben stepped in.

"Evening, Miss Delano," Ben said with a touch to the brim of his well-worn bowler hat.

"Good evening, Ben. What can I do for you?" she asked.

"I just wanted to let you know that I talked to the sheriff, and everyone in the place confirmed the story. He says he doesn't even need to talk to you, but told me to thank you for not hitting Parsons, that would have made a lot more work for him." Ben smirked as he said that last.

Ben was a good man, she thought. She'd hired him on with intent to use him as something of a bouncer for the place, but she always found herself stepping in before Ben could do that part of his job. He'd gotten used to it, and didn't make a fuss about her stepping on his toes. He just poured drinks and provided a tough face for the customers. Evie was sure that they had so few problems in the first place because of the burly Ben and his watchful eye on the girls. It was amazing what a deterrent to minor scuffles a man who was built like a bull could be.

He also never took advantage of his position with the girls, or even patronized the establishment as a customer himself. Ben was happily married, and his loyalty to his wife had been proven time and again, and Evie trusted him implicitly. Ben's wife wasn't crazy about his profession, of course, but even she couldn't deny that every single one of the girls was there by choice, and she never once questioned Ben's loyalty to her. A good woman for a good man, she thought with another sigh. Ben's smirk slipped and he tilted his head, brow coming down in concern.

"Hey, you all right?" he asked. She nodded, recognizing she'd been drifting again. She was more tired than she thought, she realized.

"Yes, thank you, Ben," she replied. "I'm sorry, I'm just tired. And sore," she added, rubbing her shoulder. "That scattergun of yours kicks like a mule!" Ben chuckled and nodded.

"She sure does," he agreed. "Kicks harder if you're on the receiving end."

"Oh," she said, reminded of the damage she'd caused, "Ben, can you get Mr. Anderson to bring some supplies for repairs as soon as possible? Rumors will be bad enough without that hole in the front wall sitting there for all the world to see."

"Already done," he reassured her. "I sent the blacksmith's boy down to pass along the message. Cost me a nickel, but he'll get the message there right quick. He's a good lad."

"Thank you, Ben," she said. He really was a fine man. She felt better knowing that he was there looking after her place, and more importantly her girls, whenever she wasn't in the building. "Go ahead and take a nickel from the cash box to pay yourself back."

"No need," he replied, his big grin widening. "It was worth the nickel to watch you take a couple of shots at Parsons. Never much liked that man, and that was before he bruised up Prudence. I hope you don't mind that I sent Ida to fetch you, instead of handling him myself. I thought this was one you'd want to handle personally, and until just before you walked in, he hadn't so much as touched her, yet."

"No fussing about that, now," she reassured him. "I saw you moving out from behind the bar when I walked in. You'd have had him well in hand, probably both hands and by the neck, in another few seconds. Prudence would have been just fine either way. Is there anything else?"

"No, ma'am. I'll check on the girls."

"Thank you, Ben."

"Ain't nothing, Miss Delano," the big man replied with another tip of his hat. Ben walked out, closing the door behind him. Evie had no idea what she'd do without him.

She couldn't believe she'd been caught woolgathering like that not once, but twice in as many minutes. She really was exhausted, but she needed to stay sharp. Being a female business owner in this part of the country was difficult enough without appearing to be addle-brained or a simpleton.

Her father would never have believed it if he'd heard she was the proprietor of her own business. Although he'd easily have believed that in doing so, she hadn't made herself rich. He'd always told her that her kind heart was a weakness. She made enough to get by, and made sure her girls and Ben were well taken care of. That was her real job, not taking advantage of their hard work to pad her bank account.

Standing and moving to her wardrobe, she reached back and undid the lacings of her dress. The lamplight flickered behind her, casting odd shadows of herself on the wardrobe and the wall above it. The shapes looked peculiar, she thought, pausing in her work. The shadows looked larger than usual and were moving strangely. Freezing perfectly still, the shadows did the same, aside from the flickering caused by the small lamp.

Wait, the lamp shouldn't be flickering, she realized. The window was closed. Her heart lurched as her mind found a name... Parsons! Spinning around, she gasped in a breath to scream.

Quick as a whip, two big hands shot out and lashed a gag around her head. Her muffled scream likely didn't carry more than a few feet, and certainly not outside the room. Her hands came up to fight him off, but his hands snapped out again, grabbing her wrists.

Effortlessly, the big man spun her around, twisting her arms around behind her. With one hand, he held both of her arms immobile as his other hand brought up a length of cord. She'd have sworn it took him less than two seconds to tie her hands securely.

Evie tried to kick out behind at her attacker, but her foot didn't reach anything, despite his being right behind her. She tried again, but still made no contact. The dangerous man's powerful arm snaked around her waist and hoisted her up as easily as a child might pick a flower.

As he tossed her on the bed, she began to truly panic. *He's going to rape me,* she thought, fighting back terror, nausea, and a disconnected sense of surrealism at the thought.

Trying again to scream, her muffled sounds were useless. As his hands moved to her feet, she kicked out again, but he was faster. One hand caught her leg, his other hand reaching out and securing the other. Almost insultingly, his one hand held both of her legs down while his other hand grabbed more cord from his belt. Another blink and her legs were bound as well.

Now fully tied, she knew she couldn't stop him from anything he chose to do. Her breath came in short, panicked gasps around the gag, and she felt her eyes begin to fill with tears. She couldn't let him see her cry, but her eyes refused to cooperate as they looked up at her attacker.

Definitely not Parsons, a detached part of her mind informed her. Evie found herself staring into a broad, gray-shirted chest. Her eyes slid up into the slate-gray eyes above, heart thumping like a drum.

She couldn't see his face, as it was covered by a tied bandana around the lower half. The upper half was shrouded in shadow from the wide-brimmed hat he wore, but his eyes…

His eyes seemed to shine like a cat's in the limited light. The piercing gray orbs were clear, sharp, and focused. Those eyes didn't belong to a coward like Parsons. They belonged to a predator.

Those steely eyes locked with hers as he leaned down close.

Despite her terror, Evie saw something surprising in his eyes, and it wasn't lust. She knew the eyes of a lustful man, better than most, thanks to her time running this business, and the eyes gazing down at her were not lustful, they were almost sympathetic.

"Darlin'," the surprisingly smooth, deep voice said, instantly ruffling her feathers. She hated being called 'darlin'. "Settle yourself down, you'll only hurt yourself against the ropes. I'm not gonna hurt you."

Evie very much doubted that, but couldn't deny that his eyes at least looked sincere. He saw her doubt, though, and clarified.

"If you don't believe me, believe this; the contract says you have to be alive and unharmed. If I hurt you, I'm out a pretty penny, and a whole lot of time."

Contract? Frowning around the gag, she was

suddenly confused. It was too soon for Parsons to have hired someone to come after her, even if he had the guts to do something that brash. He was an abusive brute, but she doubted he'd stoop to that level. But if not Parsons, then who?

"No time for that now, darlin'," he said, drawing another surge of irritation at the condescending term, "we need to get going. We've got a long ride ahead of us."

What did he mean by that? Where was he taking her? Her panic grew, but now for an entirely different reason. What was going on?

Without another word, he reached down and almost casually slung her across his shoulder. She let out a sharp burst of air as her stomach hit his broad, iron-hard shoulder.

"Sorry," he said softly as he moved toward the window.

She tried to curse at him, but the gag muffled everything, and he apparently didn't understand her references to his mother. She thrashed again as he ducked down through the window, but his grip never once slipped. He might as well have been holding her in a vice, his grip was so firm.

It wasn't painful, though, she noticed. His grip was very secure, but not one lick more than it had to be to keep her from struggling too much. He was being careful with her, she realized.

For his precious money, she thought with a growl. If they had a long ride, she had a lot of opportunities to get away. Especially if he was determined not to hurt her. That was to her advantage, not his.

Shifting his grip slightly as he leaned further out the window with her, he eased himself out, holding onto the frame with his free hand. With a sudden lurch in her stomach, he jumped, still holding her. She screamed into the gag.

They landed softer than she expected since they'd been falling from the second story window, but he had apparently landed gently on a hay bale sitting on the back of a cart that she knew for fact hadn't been there an hour before. She was impressed, despite herself.

With another light hop and one hand on the pommel, he stepped off the hay bale and into the saddle of a horse that seemed to be waiting patiently beside it, slinging her across his lap. Feet in the stirrups, he gave a low, short whistle and the horse began to move.

Without warning, he reached behind himself on the saddle as she struggled to turn her head enough to see more than the ground, the man's leg, and the horse's feet. Coming back around, he draped a heavy blanket over her, completely covering her. Nobody casually seeing him on the dark street would be able to tell she was under it, and might only assume he was carrying a large bundle.

She began thrashing again, but he made a quick

adjustment of his grip on her and she found herself barely able to move. He didn't even seem to be working hard. Evie growled again, trying to get angry rather than letting the fear win. She heard him chuckle softly above her.

"Sorry, darlin'," he said softly, "a job's a job. I've got no beef with you personally. Try to take it easy. I think I'd still get full payment if you're a bit bruised up, but frankly, I'd rather not have to hurt you at all."

For some reason she couldn't have named, she found herself believing that he really didn't want to hurt her, contract restriction or no.

For yet another reason entirely, that still didn't make her feel any better about her predicament.

Chapter Two

Evie woke to a gentle swaying sensation. As she groggily tried to collect herself, she realized she was warm and comfortable, but she wasn't lying down in a bed. It smelled nice, too, rather a faint, musky scent. That was odd, she thought. Then it all rushed back to her.

The sudden appearance of the gray-eyed man, her abduction, and his taking her covered in a blanket out of town. She'd tried to scream through the gag for what felt an eternity, before she had begun to get light-headed. Everything was already dark, thanks to the heavy blanket draped over her, but she very nearly remembered the moment that everything faded away and she passed out.

She stiffened and screamed, eyes snapping open and looking around. With a start, she realized she wasn't gagged anymore. She wasn't draped over a saddle anymore, either. He was holding her cradled in his arms, feet still bound and hanging to one side of the horse, her head against his chest.

Somehow, her arms were now bound in front

of her, rather than behind. Her scream tapered off as she looked into the slate gray eyes from the night before. The eyes again struck her as sharp, focused, and dangerous, but there was a peculiar softness there as well.

"Good morning, Miss Delano," he said, the depth of his voice sending a tingle up her spine.

Stop that, she admonished herself. He had taken the bandana off his face, though, and what she saw had her reacting in all manner of unwanted ways. His eyes were still what drew her gaze the most, but his lightly stubbled, strong jaw, almost regal nose, and surprisingly perfect lips all made a fair showing for her attention.

"Good morning, indeed," she snapped. "I have been abducted against my will by a shameless ruffian. Who are you?"

"Name's Jack Hannity," he replied, and she again clamped down hard on the tingling in her spine she was becoming afraid she'd experience every time he spoke.

"And dragged off to…" she began her tirade again, but once more tapered off, looking around. There was absolutely nothing in sight but waist-high grass and a few scrub trees. The sun was just beginning to make an appearance. That was probably what had awakened her. "Where the devil are we?"

He chuckled. "About fifteen miles south of Falls City," he replied, his honest answer surprising her.

"South of... why are you taking me south? And put me down!" Evie hated how helpless and confused she sounded, but she couldn't deny that she was exactly that, helpless and confused. It didn't make her hate feeling that way any less.

"That's where Topeka is," he said simply. He didn't put her down, but he did shift her position so she was in less contact with him. She'd take it, she thought with a frustrated sigh.

"Topeka? Why..." she asked, confused again, but only for a moment. Realization hit her and her stomach sank like a stone in the river. Her eyes went wide and she could only bring herself to whisper, "No... he wouldn't have."

"I don't know for sure which 'he' you're referring to, ma'am," her abductor said.

"My father," she answered, her voice sounding dead and hollow with her terrible realization.

"Yes, ma'am, Warren Delano. He did mention you were his daughter."

"Are you telling me my father hired you to kidnap me?" she snapped, her tone becoming uncomfortably shrill for her taste.

"No, ma'am. He hired me to bring you back home to him safely," Mr. Hannity, as she'd decided to think of him for a number of reasons, corrected. "Then I got one look at how you handled Parsons last night, and knowing your business situation, I knew there's no way in hell you'd come back with me peacefully."

"So you kidnapped me," she concluded, fighting down the flush in her cheeks as she realized he'd been in the saloon when she'd gone off the rails at Parsons.

"I suppose you could call it that," he replied calmly.

"What kind of crazy person abducts a grown woman because her father wants her to come home?" she shouted in his face. Rather than seeming bothered, the corner of his mouth quirked up in a half-smile.

"The kind that gets the job done," he answered, "whatever it takes."

"And if you'd had to shoot me to get me to come?" she asked incredulously.

"I wouldn't have had to shoot you. Besides, the contract specifically stated 'safely' as a condition of final payment."

"What if he'd hired you to kill me?" she asked, her anger continuing to build. It wasn't directed at Jack anymore, at least not primarily, but her fury with her father was nearing legendary proportions. How dare he!

"I'm not an assassin, ma'am," Mr. Hannity replied.

"Then what on earth are you?" she asked.

"A bounty hunter."

"You must be joking. Mr. Hannity, I'm no criminal."

"I know," he replied, "but you do have a bounty on your head, officially placed there by the honorable Lieutenant Governor Warren Delano for your safe return. He offered the contract to me specifically, but the bounty is officially posted, so like as not, I'm not the only person looking for you."

"Honorable my horse's arse. This can't possibly be happening," she said softly, more to herself than to him.

"Ma'am, I can't even imagine how this must have you shaken up, but you have my word, just as your father did, that I'll get you back to him safely. The more you cooperate, the easier this will be on both of us."

"And if I refuse to cooperate?" she asked indignantly. He shrugged as if it didn't matter to him either way. The horse kept walking, unconcerned with their heated conversation. At least, she thought, her side was heated. He was irritatingly untroubled by any of this.

"No skin off my back. You're far from the first uncooperative bounty I've had to drag along the trail for a few hundred miles. You are the smallest, though." She glared at him.

"Now, Mr. Hannity," she started.

"Jack," he interrupted.

"I most certainly am not calling you that. We're not that friendly. We're not friends at all."

"Suit yourself," he replied with a slight shrug. His unbending calm was infuriating.

"Now, Mr. Hannity," she tried again, "I'm prepared to offer you double what my father offered if you take me home right now."

"Three problems, darlin'. First, according to the contract, Topeka is your home and I am already taking you there. Second, you'd never be able to afford what he is offering, let alone double. Third, even if the first two weren't true, someone else would have you picked up within the week and you'd be right back here, only more likely with a fella not nearly as amiable and polite as I am. Take a moment and let the possibilities there sink in." She did so and was not reassured.

"How much is he offering?" Evie asked, her tone significantly calmer as she realized the next bounty hunter might indeed be a much more frightening opponent to deal with. She had enough trouble on her hands figuring out how to get away from Mr. Hannity who, to her annoyance, was actually being quite civil, despite his ungentlemanly abduction of her person.

"Five hundred dollars."

"What?" she exclaimed, astonished.

"Well, it's not what I'd fetch for roping in a bank robber or anything, but those are few and far between. Takes a special breed to rob a bank. A dumb breed, but a special one."

He was right. She couldn't pay him five hundred dollars, let alone a thousand. She wouldn't earn quite that much in a year. The idea that her father had offered that much was astonishing. The idea that he'd offered to hire anyone at any price to come and fetch her was both insulting and disgusting.

"I left my father of my own free will," she said, scowling at him.

"That's not what your father says, but five minutes of jawing with you, and I believe it. You don't much strike me as the docile type."

"He… what does he say, then?" she asked, genuinely curious and needing the distraction from the unreasonable pleasure his last remark had given her.

"That some 'no-good, conniving varmint' went and stole his precious baby away." Mr. Hannity chuckled at the phrasing, and she could tell her father had used those exact words. She felt her ire swell. Her father considered himself so above the common folk that for him to stoop so low as to use what he was convinced were the expletives of the less fortunate told her something else was up.

"I've been gone five years. Why now?"

"He didn't say, but I can wager a guess."

"Well?"

"Well what?" he asked, looking down at her.

She shifted position slightly in irritation, but also to circumspectly test her bonds. They were secure as ever, though not as uncomfortable as they had been when tied behind her back. She idly wondered how he'd untied her, changed her position, and retied her arms all while on the back of a moving horse and without waking her.

"Well, what's your guess?" she snapped. His expression stayed solid, but she caught a flash of amusement in his eyes. He was baiting her!

"I'd guess his efforts to shut down the coal mine outside of town have made some people a mite angry. Certain folk stand to lose a whole lot of money if he does. I reckon some of those folk may have threatened you, as a means to him, and he wants you back under his watchful eye."

Evie was quiet for a time. It would make sense that her father had made some new enemies, since he always seemed to be doing that. It also made sense that he'd try to protect her. After all, runaway or not, she was a valuable asset, and her father hated losing assets. It was a shame her mother weren't still alive. Though if she were, Evie wouldn't have left home to begin with.

"Well, all of this has been lovely, but I demand you release me."

"Demanding and getting ain't the same thing, darlin'."

"You will let me go immediately, or…" she floundered as she tried to think of some viable threat. She had none, and the amused glint in his eyes told her he knew it as well as she did. "Or I'll scream and fight you every step of the way!"

"I'd rather ride with you like this," Mr. Hannity replied, "but we can go with gagged and slung across the back of my horse if you prefer. I just thought this'd be a bit more pleasant." She brooded for a moment.

"Well at least stop calling me 'darling', you filthy dog!" she insisted. She had to win something here, even if it were meaningless.

The amusement in his eyes flared, causing what she'd first seen as cold, gray eyes to dance playfully. A flutter began in her stomach. Stop that, she mentally commanded. This was neither the time, nor the place, nor the man with whom to become attracted.

"Sure thing, darlin'."

She shouted angrily and swung her arms up, trying to hit him. He almost casually brought up one hand and caught hers at the wrists, bringing them down and pinning them to her stomach. He laughed, and her stomach fluttered again.

"I hate you," she spat, "and I'll get away."

"I know," he replied, "and no, you won't."

Jack couldn't deny he was intrigued. The only time he'd seen this woman panic was when she'd thought he intended to rape her. He'd seen the fear in her eyes and knew right away what she'd thought. Since then, her reactions to everything had been angry and sharp. The moment she'd realized he really wouldn't hurt her unless he absolutely had to, she'd gone on the offensive. Admittedly, her attacks had been mild and mostly verbal, but there it was anyway.

She was beautiful, no doubt about that, but it was that inner fire he kept seeing in her that had him watching her so closely. When she was angry, she looked about to ignite, like one more word would send her entire body up into flames. When she was calm, it felt like a deep, slow river. There was something intense about her, in any mood, and that intensity pulled at something inside of him.

He hadn't actually told her everything about her father, though. The lieutenant governor had offered the bounty to him first, but as Jack was walking out, another bounty hunter Jack knew was being escorted in to meet with Lieutenant Governor Delano.

Jack wasn't joking when he'd told Miss Delano that the next guy to come along if he let her go wouldn't likely be nearly as friendly. 'Hound' McCoy very well would do all manner of unseemly things to the poor gal.

The only thing that'd keep that man from skinning her alive for sport would be the requirement that she be returned safely. Besides, the lieutenant governor's phrasing hadn't exactly been 'safely'. He'd actually said that he wanted his daughter back in marriageable condition.

If Jack hadn't needed the money and wanted to keep clear of the wrong side of the law in Kansas, he might have hit the man where he stood. There was an awful lot that a man like Hound could do to a woman and still have her considered 'marriageable'.

Jack had at least a day or two on Hound though, since he knew he'd found her trail much faster than Hound ever could, but it would turn sour fast if they crossed paths.

Miss Delano had gone quiet after their last exchange, and other than him adjusting her position again for her comfort and the curt "thank you" he'd received, neither had said a word in over an hour. She'd begun squirming slightly, though she'd been trying to hide it, and he knew she needed to take care of some business in the brush.

"We're going to stop for a bit, near that shallow ravine. Take a rest, fix up some breakfast. Sound all right to you?" he asked her. She scowled at him, but nodded. Good enough.

He used one knee to nudge Patriot that direction, and the smoke-colored mare responded perfectly, as she always did. He was using his arms and hands more to steady Miss Delano than steer Patriot, but the horse had been exceptionally well trained, and the touches required to guide her were so simple and subtle that sometimes Jack swore the mare read his mind.

Jack guided her to a stop near one rim of the short ravine. It ran for maybe a thousand paces and was only around ten feet deep. They were right near the end, where the ground tapered almost gently down into the ravine. It'd be a good place for her to walk down into and take care of her needs while he set up breakfast.

Scooping her up like a child again, he dismounted and set her down. The sun was up clear of the horizon, but it still had a long way to go. They'd break again around mid-day and he'd see if he could get a bit of sleep.

Normally, he could doze in the saddle for hours, but it was a lot harder while he was carrying her. It had been a long night for him, though she'd slept like a baby.

He'd never carried a bounty like this before, not even the other women he'd brought in, but he'd never been hired to bring in someone who wasn't a criminal before, either. It just didn't seem right, tethering her to the saddle with a ten-foot length of rope and letting her walk, or be dragged, like he usually did.

Setting her down, he unwrapped her from the blanket and reached down, untying her feet. He was ready for her to kick, or to try to hit him from above as he untied her, but she did neither. For some reason, that troubled him.

"I'm gonna get breakfast ready. You can head on down that slope into the ravine and take care of any business that may need tending. You have three minutes."

"You can't possibly expect me to…"

"Three minutes," he interrupted, giving her the steely gaze he'd been known for, back when he run with a gang of outlaws. He'd shut up men half again his size with the ice in that stare.

She scowled, but turned and headed for the ravine. He left her arms tied in front of her, but fully expected she'd try to cut the cord with a rock or something. She might be able to do it, given time, but three minutes wouldn't be enough for that.

Besides, more than that, he expected she'd try to run and worry about the rope on her arms later. He'd been past here a few days before on the way up to Falls City and had scouted this spot well.

There was only one easy place to get back out of that ravine by someone with their hands tied aside from the slope she'd just gone down, and it was about halfway along the length of the ravine. He knew about how long it'd take her to get down that far on foot and find it, and how long it'd take him to get there on Patriot.

Jack took a few minutes to prep up a firepit and gather some wood. After setting everything up, his internal clock told him it had been about five minutes since she'd left. As expected. He mounted up and rode out toward the spot he knew she'd try to come up from.

He swung wide so she wouldn't hear him, and stopped Patriot behind a clump of bushes not far from the point she'd likely appear. He then sat down to hide and wait.

Jack didn't have to wait long, she'd made good time. He was mildly impressed.

Climbing up awkwardly, she made her way up the rock outcroppings that were evenly spaced, almost like stairs. Jack watched as she pushed her way through the bushes at the top of the ravine. Sitting behind a bush himself, she didn't see him. She'd torn her dress at some point, though not badly. Pity, he thought. It was a lovely dress.

He smiled as she looked around frantically for signs that he was around. When she didn't spot him, she turned and began running away from where he sat, and where she thought she'd left him. He stood and was about to step out when she disturbed a pheasant from its hiding place. The bird took to the air in a rush of wings.

Jack snatched the rifle from Patriot's saddle holster, aimed and fired, all in the span of a heartbeat. Miss Delano barely had time to scream and fall to one side before the bird was dropping to the ground. Jack casually walked the distance between them, picking up the felled pheasant.

She stared up at him in a peculiar blend of astonishment and horror.

"Good work, darlin'. You just flushed us up some lunch." He reached a hand down to her and grinned. "Shall we go?"

She reached for his hand like someone would reach for a dog they weren't sure was rabid or not. Taking it, he hoisted her easily to her feet and walked over to pick up the bird.

"How did you…" she asked, looking at him like she thought he was cheating at cards, then glancing back at the ravine. He shrugged.

"It's not too hard. They always run. Always."

She frowned, obviously considering this.

"And you catch them?"

"Always." Jack whistled sharply, and Patriot came trotting out from behind the bushes.

"What kind of people do you catch?" she asked, as Jack moved to the horse, tying the pheasant to a saddlebag and mounting.

He reached a hand down for her once he was seated. She hesitated, then put her two bound hands in his, and with one arm, he hoisted her easily up into the saddle across his lap.

"Cattle rustlers, mostly. A lot of that going around. The occasional bandit or murderer. Anyone with a price on their head."

"Sounds dangerous," she said, letting him steer the horse back toward the end of the ravine. He shrugged.

"What isn't, these days?" he asked.

"Lots of things," she replied.

"Such as?"

"You could be a ranch hand."

"You think that's not dangerous? Please."

"You could be a tailor," she suggested.

"I might get stabbed with a pair of shears by an angry customer," he replied, tone and expression serious. She regarded him from her side-saddle position across his lap.

"You're pulling my leg."

"Only a little," he admitted. "I once brought in a man who did exactly that. Wasn't happy with his suit, so he grabbed the shears and stabbed the tailor before trying to high-tail it out of town." At her expression, he hastily added, "The tailor lived, don't worry. I'm just saying, it's a serious risk."

She laughed, and he felt an odd sensation starting in his chest, a warmth he didn't recognize. He couldn't help but smile with her. They made it back to his prepped fire, and he lowered her down from the horse's back. He dismounted and moved to light the fire.

"Did you ever catch anyone famous?"

"Nah, can't say that I have. The famous ones usually have a lot of hunters after them, so aren't often worth the time or trouble to compete. I can catch six lesser men in the time it takes some of those hunters to wrangle one famous criminal, and make more than twice as much doing it."

"But there's no fame in that," she said with a teasing tone. "Just think if you were to catch someone really famous. Everyone would know your name!"

"I ain't after fame, darlin'. Matter of fact, I aim to avoid it if I can." He'd had fame before. Or infamy, in his case. He didn't much care for it.

"Just the money, then?" she asked with a

disdainful expression as she settled to the ground near the makeshift firepit. Jack eyed her sidelong for a moment.

"Gotta make a living."

"You could make a living as a tailor, too. And while that may carry some of its own risks, it's got to be safer than this."

"All right, I admit I may enjoy the hunt a bit, too," Jack said with a smile as he brought flint to steel several times until the spark took.

"Mm-hm," she said smugly. "You're just like all the rest. An over-sized boy who thinks he's tough, thinking it makes him a big man to carry a big gun and tussle about with dangerous men."

"I think you misunderstand, ma'am. I am the dangerous man," he replied before leaning down to blow gently on the tiny ember. If only she knew.

"You'll not fool me with that nonsense, Mr. Hannity," she retorted. "Here you are with a beautiful woman, tied and helpless, innocent as a doe, and you've not laid a single hand inappropriately on my person. I'm almost insulted."

"I'm being paid to keep you from harm, darlin'. Besides, I doubt you're that innocent. You run a house for soil-doves, after all. And who said anything about beautiful?"

Jack most certainly did think she was quite beautiful, but he'd say so on his terms, not hers.

"Careful, Mr. Hannity," she said with a scowl. "I might take it in mind to try and steal your gun and shoot you in your sleep if you keep talking about me like that. And stop calling me 'darling'."

"You wouldn't be the first to try," he said with a smile. "You would be the prettiest, though." He flashed her a wink as he put some smaller branches over the kindling that had begun to burn merrily, completely ignoring her last demand. She eyed him consideringly.

"Mr. Hannity, I don't believe you're half as dangerous as you say you are."

Jack was quiet for a long moment, his thoughts involuntarily drifting back to a time when he still rode with his brothers. Not brothers in blood, but in spirit. And then to a few years before that, when he rode with men whose only shared bond was in the love of blood and money.

Once, he was one of those men. True and fully one of them. That was a long time ago, though. He was quiet long enough that she turned to look up at him again.

"Well, if you cooperate and nobody catches up with us, you'll not have to find out, now will you," he stated, all trace of amusement and playfulness gone. He leaned down and adjusted the sticks in the small fire, adding some larger dry branches.

She watched him for several long moments, and he started to become uncomfortable with the scrutiny. Jack locked gazes with her, and she surprisingly held contact. He didn't know what she saw in his eyes after her careful study, but whatever it was clearly bothered her. Her eyes tightened slightly, the edges of her full lips turning down just a bit, and then she looked away from him.

"What's your horse's name?" she asked suddenly, after a long pause. He appreciated the obvious attempt at a subject change.

"Patriot."

"Isn't she a mare?" she asked, looking back at him curiously. He smiled slightly.

"A woman can't be a patriot?" he replied.

It was the right answer. Miss Delano turned and looked up at him with a pleased smile. He fought back the urge to smile back at her again. That was getting troublesome.

"She most certainly can, Mr. Hannity."

"Jack," he corrected.

"We're not that friendly," she said, mirroring her earlier sentiment.

"I suppose not."

"However," she added, that slightly playful tone coming into her voice again, "I am prepared to offer you two hundred dollars to simply drop me off at the next town. Then we shall be friends, and I will be more than happy to call you anything you like.

"Mr. Hannity is fine," Jack replied flatly.

She laughed again, kicking a bit of dirt his direction. Again, that unfamiliar warmth spread into his chest and he gave in, smiling at her. He pointedly ignored the warm feeling, but it troubled him a great deal.

Chapter Three

She watched him as he worked. His long, dark coat covered most of his build, though she could tell his shoulders were broad, his legs were powerful, and his stomach was flat, but she was still having trouble not staring. His stubble looked like it needed a shave again, but she found she liked the way his features were set off by the dark, short bristles. She didn't think she'd like him with a beard, though, and wondered how often he shaved.

The way he moved spoke of power and strength, and even more of control. The idea of those muscles holding her for reasons other than abduction made for a momentary fantasy before she caught herself.

Get a hold of yourself, she thought sharply. *This man has abducted you. Why on earth are you sitting here wondering what he looks like in various states of undress?*

He was striking, though, she had to admit. He was far too rough in his features to be called beautiful, but his rugged appeal was undeniable. It really was a shame they hadn't met under different circumstances, she thought. Those eyes, that voice, even the playful note in his voice when he was teasing her, all brought about feelings she hadn't had since Frank.

Maybe not even then, she admitted as Jack looked up and met her gaze, his gray eyes shining like silver in the firelight and sending her stomach into another fit of flutters.

"Beans or peaches?" Jack asked.

"What?" Evie replied, caught off guard.

"I've got canned peaches and canned beans. Which do you prefer? Or we could share if you like," he added, a peculiar note of uncertainty in his voice. "The beans will be better heated, and probably go better with the eggs I was going to fry up here, but it's your choice."

"Seems an odd choice," she said.

"Sorry I don't have more options. When we stop for lunch and dinner it'll be a bit of a better spread. Not sure what you like to eat, but I can pick up some supplies in Wellington. It's hardly a proper town, but should have a few more choices for chow. Not too many good choices in canned food, though."

"You're bringing me into a town?" The idea was so surprising it was jarring.

He snorted. "In a pig's eye."

"So…" she asked, confused again.

"So I'm going to tie you up and stash you

someplace safe while I go into town for supplies."

"What if I promise to cooperate?" she asked, putting on her best sweet voice. He gave her a look.

"My pa used to tell me a woman's word was only as good as the length of a man's belt," he started. Immediately indignant, she protested.

"What kind of ridiculous…"

"Personally," he interrupted her loudly, continuing as uf she hadn't spoken, "I've found most women to be quite reliable. Far more so than the people I usually associate with, at any rate. But the fact remains that I'm taking you someplace against your will, and if you disappear I'm out five hundred dollars, so I really have no motivation at all to trust you."

Evie scowled, not entirely mollified by his clarification of the ghastly remark.

"I do see your point, but you must understand that I find myself in a difficult position. As a woman, there are things that I need that your usual, undoubtedly male, bounties have no need for. While I do appreciate your abducting me before I had taken the time to undress so that I am not being dragged across state lines in my unmentionables, I do think you don't understand entirely what you've gotten yourself into. It will be quite unpleasant for both of us if I am not able to go into town and purchase a few things. So, I am going to make you a clear and simple deal."

It was fascinating watching the way his

expression moved as he listened to her. His stubborn expression slipped slightly into one of discomfort as she spoke of women's personal needs, then to disgust as she hinted at the inevitable results of his ignoring those needs, and then wary as she mentioned a deal.

"I'm listening," he said warily.

"I promise to cooperate with you and not make a fuss, if you take me with you into town to acquire the few things I need. That's all."

"Didn't we just talk about how it's not exactly in my best interest to trust you?" Mr. Hannity replied, raising one dark brow.

"It's not exactly in your best interests to carry me on your lap the next few days if you don't," she retorted, hoping his earlier discomfort would win over his natural mistrust. From the way he looked awkwardly away from her, she guessed the ploy might actually work, though it was a long minute before he replied.

"You cooperate, come along nice and civil-like, don't cause a ruckus or stir anything up, and I'll take you along," he finally said. She smiled, a little smugly.

"You'll have to untie me. Don't want to cause a ruckus," she echoed sweetly. He sighed, and she felt extremely pleased that she'd managed to ruffle his feathers, even if only slightly.

"When we get in sight of town, and not one second sooner. And you stay as tight to my side as if we were lawfully wed, you hear me?"

"Yes, sir," she said, raising her bound hands for a mock salute. He turned those riveting eyes back down to his work.

He drew a long, sturdy knife from the back of his belt, and she flinched in spite of herself. Mr. Hannity chuckled and brought the point of the knife down onto the top of a can in his other hand. He opened the lid with alarming efficiency and handed her the can, producing a spoon from a shirt pocket.

Evie eyed the spoon in disgust for a moment, unsure she wanted to put anything in her mouth that had been in his pocket, but couldn't argue that the spoon looked remarkably clean. With a sigh, she took the spoon and the can of peaches.

He opened the other can and took a bite with another spoon from his other pocket before turning to the small cast-iron skillet and eggs he had set up over the fire while they talked.

She watched him work in silence as she awkwardly ate her peaches with hands bound, trying to hold the can between her knees. How did a man like that come to hunt criminals? He didn't seem the usual angry, gruff type she often saw ride into town from the prairie on their way through.

Oh, he had some roughness to him all right, but he was so calm and collected, and when he laughed it made his eyes shine. He was quite charming in his irritatingly unflappable way. It was a shame she was going to have to ditch him.

Not that it mattered, she knew. She wasn't much interested in marrying, not after Frank, and certainly not to a man like Mr. Hannity. She and Frank had ridden together all the way to Falls City to get away from her father, Frank professing his undying love every step of the way.

Once in Falls City, they were going to have to wait three days for the pastor to marry them. It only took two for Evie to catch Frank in the bed of their hotel room, with the sheriff's wife.

Frank was run out of town in less than an hour, and the sheriff had a soft spot for Evie ever since, taking it upon himself to look out for her. He'd come quickly to help her deal with a few rowdy customers before she'd hired Ben. They'd become fast friends, even though the man refused to get rid of his cheating wife. It was a sore spot, though, and Evie never mentioned it.

She wondered if the sheriff had formed a posse to come looking for her, or if he'd ridden out himself. Or worse, if he'd decided she'd finally had enough of things and had ridden out on her own. No, he knew her better than that, she was sure. If he didn't, Ben certainly did, and would have demanded action. For all she knew, he was riding hard behind them coming to her rescue.

Evie hoped he wasn't riding out himself, and that he was staying at the saloon to look after her girls. She worried about them without her to keep an eye on things.

Idly, she wondered how Ben would fare against Jack. Mr. Hannity, she corrected, scowling angrily with herself for relaxing. The brute was her abductor, after all. As if reading her mind, Jack looked up at her. Seeing her scowl, he flashed an amused half-smile and went back to the eggs. Her stomach fluttered gaily, and her scowl deepened. This was bad, she told herself. Mr. Hannity had taken her against her will, he was a boorish bounty hunter, and had been hired by her father, of all people. He was the enemy.

The enemy handed her a plate of eggs, seasoned with some mixture of spices he had in a small jar. They smelled absolutely divine. Taking a bite, she involuntarily melted. They tasted even better. How could a brute hired by the devil himself make eggs so good, she asked herself?

Except he wasn't a brute, she unwillingly admitted as she took another bite. He'd been civil, at least as much as could be expected, he was well-spoken, and cleaner than any trail rider she'd seen in years. Under other circumstances, she might mistake a man like this for an educated gentleman if she met him on the street. Not a doctor or lawyer of course, but a man of some schooling and refinement. Although his manner of dress was all rough-rider, cleanliness notwithstanding.

Something about the way his duster hung draped over his broad shoulders, wide-brimmed hat shadowing his smoky eyes that practically shone out from the shadowed, handsome face…

She stopped herself once more. This man was the enemy. She couldn't believe how often she seemed to need reminding of that fact, despite the fact that they'd only met about twelve hours before. And at least eight of those hours she'd been sleeping, while for two more she'd been frantically struggling against her bonds and the extremely undignified position he'd given her, slung across his horse.

At least he made great eggs, she thought as she finished the last bite. She very nearly licked the plate, but didn't want him to think poorly of her manners. She pointedly ignored the fact that she shouldn't care one whit what her kidnapper thought of her manners. The point was, it was important to remain calm and dignified under stress, she told herself.

"You about ready?" he asked, interrupting her thoughts.

He'd finished eating and had cleaned up while she'd been sitting there woolgathering. Again. This was becoming a habit, she chastised herself.

Evie nodded as he took her plate and spoon. A quick splash of water from a canteen and a wipe from a surprisingly clean cloth, and he tucked the plates into the saddlebags, and the spoons back in his pocket. He offered her the canteen, which she took with a quick "Thank you."

She drank deeply of the cool, clean water before handing it back. A few drops trickled down her chin, and Jack reached a hand out to wipe them off for her. The fluttering in her stomach stopped at once, and a warmth spread through her belly and into her chest. He paused as he saw the stunned look on her face, his big thumb resting just below her lips for a long moment.

In a rush, he removed his hand and looked away.

"Sorry about that, ma'am, just wanted to… I mean, your hands are still bound so I thought I'd…" he cleared his throat and stood, holding a hand down to help her up. He didn't meet her eyes. She took his hand and he lifted her easily to her feet.

"It's fine, thank you," she replied coolly.

Far more coolly than she felt, she knew. His touch had sparked something in her long dormant. When his fingers had touched her face, their eyes meeting for one long second, she realized she was in trouble. A great deal of trouble indeed. She had to get away from this man, whatever it took.

Jack lifted her up in front of him on Patriot's back, pointedly avoiding her gaze. Something had happened a moment ago. Something that he not only thought would never happen again, but that was bound to raise hell in his life.

It had been a lot of years since he'd felt that warmth spreading through him. Combined with the definite spark he felt when he'd touched her, he knew he was in trouble. It had been different when he'd been tying her hands and legs, and again when he'd adjusted her position while she was sleeping.

His touch this time had been reflexive, and something he'd used to do the same way for another woman. He hadn't even thought about it, just a casual gesture. Jack had seen the drops of water on her chin and instinctively reached out.

It wasn't until he'd seen the startled expression on her face that he had realized what he'd just done. The gesture itself was casual, but the connotations of being that casual with a woman were far more intimate, and not something he cared to welcome into his world. Least of all from a confounded bounty.

He didn't speak as they rode, and thankfully neither did she. He was uncomfortably aware how much they were in physical contact, riding this way. Jack was tempted to cut her bonds early so she could ride behind him, rather than cradled across his lap as she was now.

Why didn't he just have her walk tied behind the horse like he usually did? He knew why, of course, but it didn't make him feel any better. He was just waiting for the inevitable moment when she asked him about that.

Jack's thoughts wandered as he rode, as they always did, but this time they wandered back to a time he'd been hoping to forget. A time before his band of brothers, and even before his time with the outlaws.

Jack hadn't thought of Lucy and the children in a very long time. He wondered for a moment if she'd be angry with him for that.

She would be angry with him for a lot of things, he knew, but not for that. She'd be angry he'd joined up with Jon Jarrett and his gang. She'd be angry for all the people he'd hurt. Lucy would be less angry for the Saints, his brothers, and how they'd led him away from causing harm and into helping prevent it, but she'd still have been angry that he'd shut himself off from so many things in life that had once made him happy.

He was reasonably content in his life now, but not happy. The closest he'd come to that had been riding with the Saints of Laredo, he and his brothers and their own brand of vigilante justice saving far more lives than he'd ever taken, though that number was still far bigger than he'd ever atone for. And since the Saints had gone their separate ways, all he'd managed to achieve was contentment with spending the last of his days wrangling criminals and helping to keep more people safe.

It wouldn't buy his ticket back into Heaven, but at least it would comfort him in Hell. He'd sent a lot of people there himself, and didn't expect they'd be anything less than thrilled to see him join them down there. He didn't deserve to be happy, and falling for a bounty was a sure-fire way to ensure he was tossed right back out of contentment, and down into total misery again. At least he was familiar with that state.

He'd been with a few women in the years since Lucy, but none of them had held any real emotional attachment for him. For some reason, Evelyn Delano was affecting him quite differently.

Jack hadn't realized how much time had passed as his mind drifted until Miss Delano spoke.

"I think I see the town," she said, bringing him back to the present. He turned his eyes to the horizon and saw what she was pointing out.

"Yes, ma'am. That's Wellington, all right."

"You going to untie me now, Mr. Hannity? A deal's a deal," she said imperiously, holding her bound wrists in front of his face. Her piercing blue eyes bored into his in challenge, but there was something else there he couldn't identify.

"I reckon it's about that time," he replied. Instead of untying her, however, he reigned in Patriot and lowered her to the ground. Dismounting, he untied her feet first, then her hands. The instant she was free, her eyes looked away from him, seeking an escape. She didn't run, though, he had to give her credit for that.

"Won't do you any good, darlin'," he told her. "I ride faster than you can run, and even with a good head start, you can't go anywhere I can't find you. Besides, we have ourselves a deal, if you'll recall."

"I remember," she replied sharply, her glare

clearly displaying her annoyance that he dared question her word. He read it in her eyes, though. She was planning something. Jack had no idea what, which troubled him.

"Come on, then," he said as he remounted, holding a hand down for her.

She reached up after a moment's hesitation, and he hoisted her up sidesaddle behind him. He nudged Patriot into a walk again, and she was forced to put her arms around him to keep her balance. He stifled a sigh. This definitely wasn't any better.

It still took a while to reach the town. One could see a fair distance on a clear day on the prairie, and it was a remarkably clear day. Sun shining, birds chirping, white clouds drifting lazily across the sky, and a man on a horse, riding uncomfortably with a bounty riding unbound behind him with her arms around his waist. This was not turning out to be a very good day at all, he mused.

As they rode into town, he kept his eyes sharp. This was the place they were most likely to run into Hound McCoy as he moved north tracking Evelyn. Timing was about right, too. He had stayed off the major roads all the way down here, to avoid Hound and anyone else moving north trying to find her.

He shouldn't have brought her here. He had only decided to come here for supplies because it was the nearest town off the major routes north. Close enough to be well supplied, but not so close to the coach routes or the railway that he was too likely to run into anyone looking for Evelyn.

Miss Delano, he corrected. That emotional distance was critical now more than ever. He needed to push hard and get her home before things got out of hand. If they hadn't already, he amended as Miss Delano waved and called a perky good morning to a passing cartman.

"Stop that," he told her.

"What, being polite? I told you I wasn't gonna cause a ruckus."

"You know what I mean. You're going to draw every bit as much attention like that as you would screaming your all-fired head off, and you know it," he hissed. She chuckled and he stifled another sigh. This gal was a barrel full of trouble, and it was likely to only get worse.

They rode slowly down the main road of town, looking for the general store. Spotting it, he guided Patriot toward the hitching post outside. Jack reached back and helped Miss Delano down, then dismounted himself. She smiled sweetly at him, causing his brow to furrow in suspicion.

Strutting up the few wooden steps and through the doors of the general store like she hadn't a care in the world, he had no choice but to follow. He quickly gave Patriot's reigns a single wrap around the post and tossed a coin to a boy leaning alongside the storefront.

"Bring my horse here a bag of oats and you can keep the change."

"Thanks, mister!" the boy said excitedly, racing around the side of the building.

Jack followed Evie inside. He was half afraid she'd be screaming for help by the time he came in behind her, but instead, she had begun chatting amiably with the shopkeeper, telling him what she needed. The shopkeeper was making notes as she talked. Jack eyed her suspiciously again, and walked around collecting the things he needed himself, and some more canned goods and jerky.

As she finished, the shopkeeper smiled and told her he'd round up the things on her list. Jack stood back, pretending to browse, but watching her like a hawk. As the burly shopkeeper returned, he set the goods on the counter, and Miss Delano turned to regard him expectantly. After a moment, he realized she expected him to pay for her things. He frowned and she gave him that sickeningly sweet smile.

"Sorry, but you grabbed me so fast… I mean, you swept me off my feet and took me away from my troubles so fast," she amended with a playful gleam in her eye, "that I didn't have time to even grab my purse, honey."

Jack almost laughed. If she called this behaving, they were going to have some words later. He couldn't argue, though. Not only had she been grabbed without any of her personal belongings aside from the clothes on her back, but the story that they'd run off to elope was actually a decent cover. Pretty and smart. This one was growing more dangerous by the hour. He stepped forward and put his own goods on the counter.

"Together, please," he told the shopkeeper, who threw him a wink.

Jack couldn't help but smile. As much as he hated to admit it, he suspected he was going to enjoy the next few days with her. He looked down at Evelyn while the shopkeeper tallied their purchases. She smiled up at him with that fiery, mischievous sparkle in her eyes and his grin broadened.

"That'll be seven dollars," the shopkeeper told him. His gaze snapped back in surprise.

"Seven dollars?" he asked in shock.

"Well, honey, I can't exactly go riding all the way to Topeka in this old thing, now can I? I had to get something a bit more suited to the trail," Miss Delano said, gesturing down to her torn, dusty dress. He scowled at her.

"I suppose not," he said through gritted teeth.

It would be easier to keep her tied and thrown over the back of his saddle without the petticoats in the way, he thought wryly. Her smile turned slightly smug. His mind already mulling over how to get her back for this one, he paid the shopkeeper, who handed him their wrapped parcels.

He followed her out to Patriot, who was now happily munching from a small bag of oats propped open on the ground, and he put their packages in the saddlebags. Good lad, Jack thought.

Turning, Evelyn suddenly headed across the

street. A quick glance told him the place was a saloon. What was that confounded woman up to, he asked himself. Following her, he ran a little to catch up.

"What do you think you're doing, darlin'?" he asked as he grabbed her arm. She sharply pulled her arm free of his grip.

"If you're going to drag me all the way to Topeka against my will, and turn me over to my horrible father, the least you can do is buy me a drink," she said firmly.

"I already bought you a new outfit, apparently!" he snapped.

Jack couldn't believe how well she was able to get to him. He'd had a reputation among the Saints for being steady as a rock. This woman could dig under his skin quicker than a starving tick. He reminded himself of his earlier thought about how much he'd enjoy this trip, and uncertainly amended it. She was getting under his skin, but he kind of liked that, too.

"Well, then a quick applejack won't be but a few more pennies," she said, walking into the saloon. He shook his head in amazement. Abducted or no, this woman was certainly not going to go quietly. Unable to keep down his smile, he followed her in.

"Afternoon," she said to the barkeep as the man came over.

The room was crowded. The place must serve

lunch, too, Jack thought. He instinctively scanned the other patrons, noting who was obviously carrying, and who else was likely to be.

"What can I get you?" the old barkeep asked.

"Applejack, please," she told him. He nodded and looked at Jack with a questioning brow.

"Two fingers of gut warmer," Jack said. The old barkeep nodded, and moved off. Evelyn looked at Jack with a smile.

"A whiskey man, hmm?" she asked.

"Sometimes. The stuff around here is so watered down it barely counts, though. Gotta keep sharp around you," he answered, handing a few coins to the barkeep as he returned with their drinks.

She laughed pleasantly, and the warmth spread through his body. It was such an easy, melodic sound. He got the impression she did that a lot when back home, and he couldn't deny he liked that thought. She raised her glass in salute.

"That you do, Mr. Hannity."

"Jack."

"We ain't that friendly," she retorted, but she said it with a sparkle in her eyes.

She sipped her applejack and made a contented sigh. He smiled and downed his whiskey in one quick shot. Sure enough, the whiskey was watered down enough it probably wasn't possible for even Evelyn to get drunk on it. He'd had stronger breastmilk as an infant, he had no doubt.

Frowning slightly in disappointment, he looked

around as someone shifted a chair. Just someone readjusting, he noted, and turned back. Evelyn was whispering to the man on the far side of her on the bar.

"Hey," Jack got out before the man's eyes went wide and he jumped to his feet from the rickety stool he'd been perching on.

"This woman's been kidnapped!" shouted the man, pulling Evelyn aside and stepping up to Jack. Without another word, the man took a swing at him.

Quick as a snake, Jack leaned back as the man's punch went harmlessly past. His own fist snapped up like a steam piston, and connected resoundingly with the man's chin. The man went down without a sound.

The sound of chairs being pushed back all around the room caused Jack's gaze to quickly scan the room. Almost every man in the place had stood and was moving toward him. He locked eyes with Evelyn, whose eyes sparkled with mischief.

His gray eyes darkened as his mind slipped into the place where the demons lived. It was here that Jack became truly dangerous. Her smug expression faltered. If she wanted a show, she was about to get one, he thought. Jack Hannity was mighty handy with a gun, but there wasn't a better brawler this side of the Mississippi.

Chapter Four

Evie didn't even resist as he led her back outside and mounted up with her on Patriot's back. She had never in her entire life seen anything like what had just happened inside that saloon, and it had stunned her into total compliance.

Jack had been more than good. It had taken him almost no time at all to drop half the men inside that saloon and send the other half running out the door for their own safety. After which he'd calmly put a few more coins on the bar to pay for damages, grabbed her wrist, and walked her out the door. Jack was completely unscathed.

Nobody had even drawn a gun, though she had seen a few of the men with pistols strapped to their belts. She could only assume that nobody was willing to gamble their lives that his skill with his fists wasn't rivaled by his skill with a six-shooter.

He had moved between chairs and tables and men like a dancer, making sure nobody could surround him as he handily tore the place apart, one patron at a time. It was awe inspiring, and more than a little terrifying.

Glancing down at his knuckles, she could see the blood, but she wasn't sure how much was from his knuckles, and how much came from the men he'd been using those knuckles on.

Evie looked up at his face. He wasn't looking at her, just straight ahead as they made their way toward town. He was pushing Patriot faster than he had before, but not quite enough to make it obvious they were rushing.

Jack looked totally unconcerned and relaxed, but she could tell by his pushing Patriot and by the way he kept casually glancing around that he was trying to get out of town before the law showed up. For some reason, she felt guilty. She should feel no such thing, she knew. He had kidnapped her, and she'd made an effort to escape. But she still felt a little guilty.

"Are you hurt?" she asked him, voice soft and apologetic.

"No," he replied flatly.

"I shouldn't have done that," she admitted.

"No, you shouldn't."

"You looked like you enjoyed that," she justified. The look he gave her was dark and dangerous.

"Lot of good men got hurt in there. Didn't need to be."

"You actually feel bad for it?" she asked, a little surprised.

"I don't like hurting people," he said, tone softer than she'd expected.

She studied his eyes. There was a sadness there that went far deeper than just the saloon back there. Jack Hannity had a past, she realized. One that he wasn't comfortable with. It made sense, in a way. A man who lived a life like Jack did wasn't likely to have started out there and stayed because he liked it.

"I'm sorry," she said sincerely.

"Me too. I hope you learned from that, though. I gave my word to your father I'd bring you back safely. I always keep my word. Always." His voice was as cold and unyielding as iron. "No matter what stupid stunts you try to pull, no matter what ruckus you raise, no matter how you try to get away, you can't stop me from finishing this contract. All that's gonna happen is that people will get hurt. You understand me?"

"Yes," she said simply, her tone sincerely contrite and humbled.

She did understand that, more from the tone of his voice and the look in his eyes as he said that last than from the words themselves. No matter what softness and playfulness she'd seen in brief flickers before, this was a man not to be trifled with.

The darkness she'd seen flare to life in his eyes when he'd looked at her before the fight had been beyond terrifying. They were, as she'd seen when he'd first grabbed her, the eyes of a predator.

There was more to him than that, though, she

knew. She'd seen it. She'd seen the sadness, seen the dancing eyes when he laughed, had seen the look in his eyes when he'd touched her so casually. The darkness terrified her, but it also added another layer to this growing enigma of a man that she was drawn to more strongly by the moment.

The sound of several gun hammers being locked back caused both of them to freeze. Jack eased Patriot to a stop. Looking over, she saw three men, rifles all leveled at Jack. Evie's heart leaped into her throat.

"Two fingers," the man with the sheriff's badge said firmly. Jack's hands moved slowly and carefully. With thumb and forefinger, he reached down toward his gun. "Easy," cautioned the sheriff.

Jack didn't use those two fingers to draw and drop the gun, however. He pulled something else from the belt beside it, holding it out for the sheriff to see. Evelyn was stunned to see it was a badge.

"Afternoon, sheriff," Jack said cautiously. "I'm a duly appointed deputy in the states of Kansas, Missouri, Nebraska, and Colorado, and a registered bounty hunter. This here is a legally registered bounty collection."

"Word is she's a kidnapping victim. And that you assaulted about twelve of my townsfolk, sending another dozen running afeared for their lives," the sheriff growled, looking Jack over like he was trying to decide if he could have actually done so single-handedly.

"Self defense, sheriff. The bounty here tried to incite a riot by declaring herself a kidnapping victim, to try and escape lawful custody. I was forced to defend myself. Your fine townsfolk weren't much inclined to discuss the matter calmly. I'm sure witnesses told you I never drew down on anyone. Nor did anyone draw on me, so it stayed nice and friendly, a gentleman's brawl. No harm done, and I even paid for the damages, you can check that with the good bartender."

The sheriff eyed Jack suspiciously, then looked to Evie.

"She don't look like any kind of criminal to me," he stated, spitting tobacco juice into the dirt.

"No sir, she sure doesn't. She's not a criminal, she's wanted for her protection by the lieutenant governor of the state of Kansas. I'm bringing her directly to his custody on matters of security."

"All this true, ma'am?" the sheriff asked Evie. She wasn't sure what to say. She nodded uncertainly.

"Let's see the warrant," the sheriff said, relaxing somewhat, but clearly not yet convinced.

Jack slowly reached into an inside pocket on his coat and pulled out a folded sheet of paper. Unfolding it, he held it down to the sheriff. The sheriff uncocked his rifle, but the other two kept theirs ready, if no longer aimed directly at Jack.

Stepping forward, the sheriff took the paper and studied it closely. After a moment, she realized he wasn't reading it. He probably couldn't read, she thought. She recognized her father's signature and the state seal on the document, though. That alone should be enough to verify Jack wasn't lying.

Evie had meant to get the men in the saloon to hold him so she could escape, not to get him arrested or shot by the sheriff.

After a long moment, the man handed the document back to Jack, who folded it neatly and returned it to his coat.

"Maybe I'd better hold you both and send a telegraph to Topeka and ask about this."

"Sheriff, I appreciate your diligence, I truly do, but licensed bounty hunters and duly appointed deputies are not the only ones looking for this woman. She is wanted for her protection by the lieutenant governor, after all. I'm afraid in the time it'd take to send that message and get a reply, someone less pleasant than I am will come along looking to take her off both our hands, and maybe not all in one piece. Besides that, holding us would be interfering with a government order, and delaying a matter of state security. That'd be enough to mean your badge, sheriff, and I don't want that any more than you do. We're both officers of the law, after all. I'd like to take my charge here and just be on my way, no harm done. You've seen all the documents are in order."

"Well, I suppose so," the man said hesitantly. "Maybe I'll just telegraph anyway, just to let them know you're coming."

"By all means, sheriff. Tell them I'll be in Topeka in three days, if I don't run into any more trouble," Jack said, giving Evie a pointed look. She looked away. That comment was apparently enough to convince the sheriff.

"All right, then. Boys, lower the guns. Sir, you're free to go."

"Thank you, sheriff. Good day," Jack replied with a tip of his hat. He nudged Patriot back into a walk.

Neither of them spoke until they were clear of the town's limits.

"Why didn't you want to get stopped by the sheriff if this is all completely legal?" Evie asked curiously.

"Takes time, for starters. Small town sheriffs can get finicky too, so that may not have gone as smoothly as it did. Which brings up the trouble that he now knows we came through here, so anyone else trying to track you down has a solid trail through this place to follow us. Won't help that half the men in town have now seen the both of us too, thanks to that mess in the saloon."

"I am sorry," she said again.

"I know," he replied. She was quiet another long minute before speaking.

"Do you really think anyone dangerous would be coming after me?" It hadn't struck her until she'd seen the warrant that she actually might be in legitimate danger.

"Yes, I do. So does your father, or he wouldn't be offering five hundred dollars for you to be brought back to his care. You might well be in a whole lot of danger. Your father's latest enemies, maybe. Other bounty hunters for sure. At least one that I guarantee you don't want to be the man who finds you."

"What will happen if they catch us?"

"You'll just have to hope I can draw faster than they can."

Evie shut her mouth and thought about that for a long time as they rode. Her father really had made some people angry enough that he thought she was at serious risk. Five hundred dollars was a lot of money, and she was probably an easy mark, so it was bound to draw some of the more dangerous bounty hunters.

She hoped nobody caught up with them, but she was suddenly very glad she was with Jack. She caught a whiff of him and winced.

"Ugh, what is that smell?" she asked. His normally appealing musky scent seemed to have suddenly gone sour.

"Tequila. Someone threw a bottle at me in the saloon. The bottle didn't hit me, but I got splashed pretty good. I was meaning for us to take a room in town and rest Patriot for a while, but there's a creek another few miles out that'll work fine for a rest, lunch, and some quick clothes-washing."

"That sounds good," she said.

Spending so much time sitting awkwardly tied on his horse wasn't exactly the most comfortable way to travel. Though she appreciated that he hadn't yet tied her up again. That brought a thought to mind, however.

"How do you usually transport your bounties? I don't reckon you carry them on your lap," she pointed out with a smile, hoping to ease the tension.

It worked, and he chuckled. His rich, deep voice sent that now-familiar flutter through her stomach. She hated that she loved that so much.

"No, I don't reckon I do. Truth be told, most of them I lash to the saddlehorn and give them just enough lead rope that they can either walk behind Patriot or get dragged. Their choice, of course."

She stared at him as she pictured that. For a moment she didn't believe him and wondered if he were pulling her leg, but he looked completely serious. Evie certainly wouldn't put it past him.

"Why in the Sam Hill would you carry me that way, then? And all night, too?"

"Didn't seem proper, making you walk. And all night, too. You're not a criminal, after all." He smiled down at her. "I might be a bounty hunter, but I'm not a complete cad."

"No, I suppose you're not," she mused, teasingly. He chuckled again. "Kind of you to carry me all night, though."

"Nah, that was easy. It was the snoring that was a real burden."

"What?!" she snapped indignantly.

"I'm only joshing with you," he laughed.

"I should say so!" she said sharply.

"Your snoring isn't that bad at all."

"You really are a cad!" Evie said, giving him her most disgusted look. He laughed again and she found herself relishing the sound. It sounded warm and bright, deep and rich. They rode quietly for a few more minutes.

"Be a good chance to get out of that dress," he said suddenly.

"I beg your pardon?" Evie said, shocked.

"Into your riding getup that I so generously bought for you back in town. I'll be by the creek washing up my shirt and coat, so you can go into the trees beyond the creek and change out of that torn dress."

"You'd trust me out of your sight?" she asked, incredulously.

"Well, you wouldn't make it a mile out before I caught you out here. Besides, I wouldn't want you to change while still in my sight."

"How considerate of you," she said dryly. He chuckled.

"I just meant that it would be uncomfortable for you, and ungentlemanly of me. I didn't mean to imply you weren't worth watching undress."

She eyed him, unsure whether to take any of that as insulting. His face looked mildly amused, but his gray eyes were dancing again.

"Every time I start thinking you really aren't a boorish brute and might be a gentleman after all, you say something like that to change my mind," she said, settling on mild offense as the proper reaction.

"Can't be too much of a gentleman and survive long out here. I do what I can, though."

He really was a fascinating man, she thought. A gentleman bounty hunter. She'd never heard of such a thing.

"What did you do? Before, I mean?" she asked. She hadn't intended to ask, but suddenly the thought had come upon her again and she couldn't stop the question from rolling out.

"Before hunting bounties?" he asked. She nodded. He took a deep breath and sighed.

"Broke a few laws."

"I'm shocked," she said, her voice dripping with insincerity.

"Now, now," he chided. "It isn't what you'd think. I rode with a group of men who dealt with dangerous men before they could hurt other people."

"'Dealt with'?" she quoted, questioningly. "Isn't it the responsibility of the lawmen to deal with dangerous men?"

"It is. But sometimes the law is too slow, and people get hurt while waiting for the paperwork." His tone had taken on that note of sadness she was starting to recognize.

"So you were a... vigilante?" she asked. He

nodded.

"We used to ride near Laredo. Handled a lot of very dangerous men while the law was still deciding on what they could be charged them with. Saved a few lives. Locals started calling us saints. The name stuck, and we were local legends for a few years. The Saints of Laredo." Jack chuckled at the memory, but his tone remained slightly sad.

"What happened?" she asked.

He didn't answer for a long time, and she thought he'd decided to just stop talking altogether, until he opened his mouth and spoke again.

"I see the creek ahead," he said simply. She sighed. Well, it was a start.

Jack guided Patriot toward the treeline. Most of the surrounding landscape was grassland, but there was a clear line of trees outlining what she assumed was the stream he was talking about.

He eased her down and dismounted himself before gesturing toward a thicker clump of trees some distance downstream.

"Might be best to change down there," he said. "Should be a mite more private. I'm going over here to wash my shirt and coat, and can meet you back here soon enough." Jack handed her the brown paper package that contained her new outfit, gestured one more time, and then walked straight toward the stream's edge.

Evie hesitated a moment, then turned and began walking toward the tight cluster of trees he'd indicated. The dappled sunlight played through the leaves overhead in a remarkably pleasant manner. It would be easy to spend a day or two right here, she thought. As she walked, she looked out toward the open plains just visible outside the tree line.

For a long moment, she entertained the idea of running again, but cast a look back at Jack. He had just reached the water's edge and removed his coat. The upper part of his shirt sleeves hugged his muscular arms tightly as he crouched down and reached forward toward the water.

I can convince him. I can convince him to let me go. But do I want to? The thought troubled her more than she cared to admit. It wasn't just the threat of danger he'd assured her was real, though she certainly felt a good deal safer with him around.

It was more than that, though. She not only wanted to convince him to take her back home, she wanted to convince him to stay with her, just for a while.

There was something about him that drew her like a moth to a flame. Like the moth, this attraction would probably kill her, in the end. Jack wasn't a local dandy, or even a local tough. He was a dangerous man, a rover and a hunter. The man chased killers for a living, she reminded herself as she stepped into the thickest part of the cluster of trees. Looking back, she couldn't see him anymore.

Thoughts tumbling over one another, she began untying her dress. She was the daughter of a politician, run away with a man and cast aside for another woman, only to find herself running a brothel just across state lines from her father's control. They would make a terrible match. She couldn't stop entertaining the idea, however.

Every time she thought about running, she heard Jack's laugh in her mind, pictured his gray eyes dance, and was captured by that sly half-smile he threw when he'd gotten the best of her… again. He was a challenge, and she knew that was part of his appeal. She was notorious for ruffling feathers, and he was remarkably unruffleable. Evie smugly acknowledged that she'd done it a time or two though, which made her feel inordinately pleased.

The challenge wasn't all of it, though. Not by a long shot. The sadness in his eyes from time to time pulled at her heartstrings every bit as much as his laugh did. Even the dangerous, predatory gleam those stunning eyes took on when he was ready to fight sent a peculiar thrill coursing through her veins. And that deep, rich voice… she sighed as she thought about it. She truly had never experienced anything like it.

Changing into the britches and shirt, she did up the last of the buttons and pulled on the soft boots, then gathered up her torn dress. She probably should just burn the thing at this point. Her trek through the ravine to try and escape had not only been difficult, but very dirty. The dress was torn and stained, and was completely ruined. She vowed to make Jack buy her a new one. She'd have to trick him into it again, like she had with the britches and boots. Evie smiled at the thought of trying to best him again.

Heading back toward Patriot, she noticed he wasn't back yet. Again, she cast a glance toward the tree line but never stopped walking toward Patriot. When she got there, she dropped the dress on the ground and patted the mare, who nickered softly and happily at her touch. She was a beautiful mare.

Looking up toward the stream, she saw Jack. He was still crouched by the edge of the water, but he had his shirt off. His jeans hugged his upper legs and backside like they'd been molded to fit him. Jack's back was toward her, and the tanned skin along his back and shoulders flexed and moved as he worked his gray shirt in the water, a bar of lye soap in his hand. His muscles were clearly defined, like they'd been chiseled by a sculptor. A master sculptor, she thought as she felt that warmth rush through her entire body.

The only flaws were the scars. There were several, though not enough to mar the impressive shape of his muscles. Two looked like bullet wounds. The others could have been knife scars, or maybe from a lash. She couldn't really tell which, and it didn't much matter. The physical signs of his past pain seemed to reflect the sadness in his voice and eyes when he started to talk about days long gone.

Turning slightly, Jack rose from the streamside. He wrung out the shirt, and she couldn't stop staring as she watched the muscles on his chiseled arms work. The warmth was turning quickly to heat, she realized uncomfortably. Reaching high, he hung his shirt on a branch beside the coat, stretching his powerful form in a manner that caused her breath to hitch.

For an instant, her thoughts turned to a fantasy of being held in that grip, wrapped in those arms, her body up against the warmth of his chest. Then Jack turned toward her, and she froze in an uncomfortable blend of embarrassment and awe. His chest and stomach were every bit as impressive as his back and shoulders, if not more. *Breathe, Evie,* she thought sharply. He eyed her a moment, and she spent three terrified seconds irrationally wondering if he had somehow seen her thoughts.

Jack walked up the bank toward her, and frowned at her. There was no way he could miss the rosy flush of her cheeks. She was glad of the mare standing between them, though she couldn't have said exactly why.

"If it bothers you to see a man unclothed, you can look away, you know," he said suddenly, misinterpreting her flushed cheeks to be from an uncomfortable embarrassment. He was partially right, but not for the reasons he gratefully seemed to have misread.

"A man with his shirt off doesn't trouble me,

Mr. Hannity," she said tartly, trying to cover her embarrassment. "I'm simply a bit parched. Where is the canteen?"

He regarded her another moment, then reached into the bag and pulled it out, handing it to her across Patriot's back before beginning to undo the straps of the bags, and then the saddle.

"We're staying a while?" she asked.

"I reckon Patriot's been walking all night and half the day carrying double. She's earned a good rest. Besides, I need to wait for my shirt to dry, and we need to get some chow."

"You don't have two shirts?" she asked innocently. He gave her a half smile of amusement.

"Yes, ma'am, I do. But the other is my Sunday shirt," he winked as he said that last and the warmth, which hadn't eased one bit with his approaching her still shirtless, flared again.

"Sunday shirt? Why, I don't believe you've ever been to church a day in your life, Mr. Hannity," she replied, frantically trying to get her body back under her control. He chuckled as he lifted the saddlebags easily off the mare's back and setting them beside a nearby tree.

"An old friend of mine used to call it a Sunday shirt. Just means it's the shirt I save for special occasions."

"Why did he call it a Sunday shirt, then?" she asked, unable to keep her gaze from slipping down the length of his flawlessly sculpted chest and taut stomach every time he looked away to what he was working on. Jack lowered the saddle to the ground and came back up for the saddle blanket.

"He was a preacher. Or became one shortly after we parted ways. He kept telling me he hoped to see me on Sunday in that shirt."

"Did he ever?" she asked, watching as he pulled a brush and an apple from the saddlebag. He chuckled again. Stop that, she chided herself as that buzzing thrill ran through her body again. Her cheeks felt hot.

"Can't say that he did. God and I have a different kind of relationship, darlin'. He thought God could be found in churches and that book of his. I never did find much sign of God in places like that."

"Where have you found signs, then?" she asked, genuinely curious.

He handed the apple to Patriot, who eagerly snatched the treat as Jack began running the brush down her dusty, sweaty coat. Something about the way he touched and handled Patriot sent a different kind of warmth through her.

"Oh, all over, I'd say. In a warm sunset, in the richness of a good bourbon whiskey, in the howling of the coyotes on a lonely night. Just about any place a man can find a bit of peace."

"That's remarkably poetic," she admitted, emotionally moved despite herself.

"Don't go spreading that around," he said with

a playful smile. "No bounty is going to be afraid of a man who spouts poetry to pretty ladies in the middle of the day." Her almost-cooled cheeks flushed again.

"Pretty ladies?" she asked, before she could stop herself.

Jack paused, his eyes dancing in amusement in that infuriating way that set her heart fluttering, leaning on his arms across Patriot's back.

"Now don't go getting a big head, darlin'. You're not the prettiest I've ever seen."

"How do you manage to ruin every compliment?" she asked in mild annoyance. He grinned.

"Can't have you thinking we're friends, now," he pointed out. "After all, I am the one taking you back to dear old pa without your consent."

"Now you've really ruined it," she said with a scowl. He shrugged and went back to brushing.

"Sorry, darlin'. Gotta keep some rules in place. Never get too friendly with a bounty."

"Then why do you keep telling me to call you Jack?" she asked.

"Because every time you call me Mr. Hannity, I keep looking around for my pa, though he's been dead more years than I care to recall. It's downright unsettling."

"You're a peculiar person, Mr. Hannity," she pointed out. His smile told her the observation was unnecessary, as he was already fully aware of that fact.

"That's for absolute certain, darlin'."

He continued brushing Patriot as she turned and walked past him toward the saddlebags where the pheasant had been tied. If it was lunch time, the least she could do was help get things started. She wasn't certain if it bothered her more that he insisted on calling her 'darling', or that it didn't bother her half as much as it had just a few hours ago.

Evie was several steps past him when she turned and glanced back at him, hoping for another look at those powerful shoulders, but instead, she found him looking at her. Specifically, at the back of her britches.

His eyes snapped up to hers the moment she turned her head, and he actually looked a touch embarrassed. He had been enjoying the view, she realized! With a smug smile, she cocked one hip to the side, looking at him back over her shoulder.

"Not the prettiest?" she asked coyly.

"Ain't the ugliest, either," he replied with a wink. She couldn't help it. She laughed.

Chapter Five

A few hours later, with a full stomach and the sun dancing playfully through the leaves above, Jack was dozing under a tree. Evelyn was making a futile effort to do some repairs on her dress under a nearby tree while Patriot grazed on the thick grass.

She had helped him cook lunch, and they'd bantered back and forth like old friends. Nothing serious had come up, which he was grateful for. She had a knack for getting him to start opening up, something he hadn't done in a long time. She had talked a bit about Ben, the bartender and bouncer at her establishment, sharing some funny stories about customers who'd crossed him.

It still struck him as odd that a woman like Evelyn had ended up opening a brothel. She was so proper. It seemed such an odd deviation from the life path she'd likely started on, as the daughter of a prominent politician. Her family would obviously have had money, and just from the way she spoke, he knew she'd had a fair amount of schooling. He wasn't willing to ask about what brought her to leave her father and that comfortable lifestyle to end up running a house of ill repute in a two-horse town like Falls City.

If he asked, he suspected she'd tell him, and he was already getting too close to her. It was hard not to, though. He loved teasing her, and loved the challenge of trying to keep one step ahead of a gal as sharp and fiery as Evelyn was. She gave as good as she got, which he found both frustrating and incredibly attractive.

They had a few more days of riding, and they'd been on the road only one full day's ride, though most of that had been while she'd been sleeping at night. If it kept up like this, he'd have a hard time letting her go when they reached her father.

As he'd watched her help prepare lunch in those britches, he also couldn't argue that his attraction had other components as well. He admitted it had been some time since he'd been with a woman. Far longer than he recalled, in fact, but this was different. With her, the interest wasn't for a quick tousle in the hay. He wanted more than that. He couldn't have even that much with this woman, though. She was a bounty, and he had a contract to fulfill.

It wouldn't be fair to her to lead her along. He really did have to keep the distance between them. It was so easy to slip with her. So easy to forget that he was supposed to be alone, that he was supposed to hate the world for what it had done to him. Lucy, forgive me, he thought as he slipped into sleep.

He was awakened a few hours later by the sound of hoofbeats. He'd rolled to his feet and drawn his gun before he was fully awake. As he took in the situation, he found himself watching Evelyn's back fading into the distance as she rode off on Patriot.

That double-crossing snake, he thought angrily. She'd promised to behave herself, and he'd again believed her. It was far too easy to relax his guard around that blasted woman. He'd even let her talk him into not binding her hands and legs while he and Patriot rested, since they'd both been up all night. He holstered his gun and ran for his shirt and coat. That girl was going to spend the rest of this ride tied and gagged, he vowed.

Once he caught her, that was. Patriot was a rare Morgan, and a natural-born runner, one of the reasons she was such an exceptional horse. Once she got it into her mind that it was time to really run, she was lightning and could run that way for miles.

He whistled sharply, and Patriot in the distance started to slow. Miss Delano kicked her faster again. Jack cursed under his breath, snatching his shirt and coat from the branch, and trying to throw the shirt on as he ran. Patriot liked her, he grumbled to himself, or she'd never have ignored his whistle to follow her commands instead. That just figured.

Another pair of hoofbeats approaching caused him to duck back deeper into the underbrush. A brown mustang tore past, heading after Miss Delano. On the stallion's back was a face Jack recognized and wished he hadn't ever seen again; Hound McCoy.

His angry cursing vanished in a sudden surge of panic. If Hound caught up with her, Jack wasn't likely to get her back. Patriot or Miss Delano, he amended. He leaned heavily into his run, dropping the heavy coat.

If she was smart, and heard Hound coming, she'd circle back around to come back to his protection. He prayed she was that smart. Patriot could handily outrun Hound's mustang, but not forever. She was already tired, her rest interrupted, and sooner or later Hound would catch her.

Jack ran. Moving out away from the treeline, he was able to run faster, not having to push through or over underbrush. He could see them in the distance. Hound was already gaining on her. Patriot needed the rest Evelyn had stolen from her. His anger was coming back.

In the distance, Patriot began to circle wide into the plain. Good girl, he thought. She must have spotted Hound and was coming back. Whether on her own or at that confounded woman's urging, he didn't know, nor did he care just then. Just come back to me, he thought urgently.

As they circled around, they lost a lot of ground to Hound, who cut the circle tightly. Jack moved back to just inside the treeline. If she was smart enough to turn Patriot, maybe she'd be smart enough to come close to the trees. He kept running, but kept a sharp eye on the approaching pair. It was going to be close, he knew. Hound was gaining fast. Patriot didn't have much left in her.

He picked his spot and changed angles. With a running step up onto a fallen log, he leaped out of the treeline, catching Hound squarely on the side. Both men tumbled over the side of the horse to the ground.

The pair fell apart as the landed, and both rolled to their feet, guns drawn and hammers clicking back at almost the exact moment. Only a few feet away, they both stared coldly into one another's eyes.

Jack didn't mind so much that Hound was competition. He minded that Hound was almost single-handedly giving the profession of hunting bounties a terrible reputation. If a Wanted poster said "dead or alive", Hound always brought them in dead. Always. And usually only left just enough intact to be positively identifiable. The man was no better than the bounties he chased, and a far cry worse than most of them. The only difference was that Hound was being legally paid for his atrocities.

"Afternoon, Hannity," Hound said, his tobacco-stained teeth glinting sickly in the sunlight.

"Hound," Jack replied coldly.

"Been a while," Hound said amiably, but his eyes were dark and eager.

Hound wouldn't hesitate to kill Jack, if he

thought he could pull the trigger faster. He wasn't sure he could, or he'd have done it already, Jack knew. It would be close. If it had been his old friend and Saints brother Thomas Jarrett, Hound would have run the moment he'd laid eyes on him. Nobody was faster than Jarrett. The man was a legend. Jack was very good, but so was Hound.

"This bounty is mine," Hound said.

"Like hell," Jack replied. "I've had her since Falls City."

"Looks to me like you lost her. Along with your horse," Hound said with a mocking sneer. Jack grit his teeth. If word of this got out, it would seriously damage his credibility in the business.

"She's a slick one," Jack agreed.

"I'll find out soon enough." Hound's mocking sneer turned lecherous and Jack felt a surge of rage like he hadn't felt in years rush through him.

"Ride away, Hound. Ride away now and I promise I won't kill you today," he snarled through his teeth.

"Not in much of a position to make demands, Hannity."

The pair slowly circled, guns trained on one another with rock-steady arms. Each watched closely for the barest interruption of focus to make their move. Neither gave any.

"I ain't demanding," Jack clarified, "I'm simply stating the facts. If you don't ride away right now, you won't ride away at all."

"Awful big talk from a man whose bounty stole his horse. I reckon she batted those long lashes at you and you broke like a yearling foal."

Jack was ashamed to admit that wasn't far from the mark. She'd caused him to lower his guard not once, but twice in a single day. Never again, he vowed. Once he'd killed Hound, he'd track her down and they'd ride to Topeka with her bound and gagged every step of the way.

"Looks like it's your horse that was trouble breaking. Fool mustang is probably across state lines by now," Jack taunted, hoping to cause Hound to glance around for his horse. He wasn't lying, the mustang had run straight off into the plains the instant Hound had come off his back. Jack didn't blame him.

The sound of a nearby gunshot rang out, and Jack pulled the trigger reflexively as pain exploded in his left arm. Hound dropped like a sack of grain, a bullet in his skull.

Jack spun toward the sound of the gunshot, pushing the pain in his arm out of his mind so he could focus on the problem at hand. He'd been shot, but not by Hound. Hound's gun had still been aimed at Jack's head. If he'd fired, Jack would be dead.

To his astonishment, Evelyn stood not far from him, just inside the treeline, holding his rifle. She looked horrified, and dropped the rifle in shock. Jack holstered his gun with a snap as the truth sank in.

"You shot me!" he yelled in a fury. He stormed toward her. She took an involuntary step back. "You crazy woman, you stole my horse and then shot me with my own gun! What is wrong with you!"

"I'm…" she stuttered, stepping back again. She looked terrified. "I'm so sorry, I… I missed.. I was aiming for… I wanted to… Oh, I'm so sorry, are you all right?"

"What in the nine hells makes you think I'm all right? You put a bullet in my arm!" he looked at the arm, and the blood now soaking the torn sleeve. He could tell from the tear in the fabric that it had only been a glancing blow. It'd probably still take a few stitches, he thought. He knew from the amount of blood, if nothing else.

"I didn't mean to," she said, tone soft and pitiful.

"Did you mean to steal my horse? Did you mean to ride off unprotected and put yourself in plain sight of that killer?" he gestured angrily back toward Hound's body. She winced as she followed he gesture.

"Is he…" she asked, reluctantly.

"If he's not, he'll have one bear of a headache in the morning," Jack snapped back.

"You killed him?" she asked, voice barely above a whisper.

"Either I killed him, or he'd have killed me and ridden off to do the Good Lord knows what to you before dumping your barely-breathing body on your daddy's front steps for his reward."

"I've never seen anyone killed before," she said softly. His anger eased, though only slightly.

"I'm sorry you had to see it this time." Jack paused, looking in her eyes. He took a deep breath and sighed, doing his best to cool his rage. The pain in his arm wasn't helping. "It wasn't your fault," he assured her. "Hound would have found us by the creek, either way. It would have been him or me then, too. You can blame your father for sending him after you, if you have to blame anyone."

"He sent you after me, too," she said, finally looking away from the body in the grass.

"Lucky for you, or Hound would have found you first." Jack moved to Hound's body, slipping the man's gun into the back of his belt. A quick search of his pockets turned up a few dollars and a pocketknife, all of which Jack took.

"Are you robbing him?" she asked, aghast.

"It's not like he needs any of this," Jack pointed out. "Besides, if I don't, next man to come along sure will."

"I don't think that makes me feel any better. Are you just going to leave him here?"

"You want to carry him with us?" Jack asked, eyeing her.

"Of course not! I just thought… I don't know, maybe we should bury him."

"It's better than he deserves," Jack growled,

looking back at the body.

"Everybody deserves that much," she said softly. Jack took a long breath to steady himself again. She was impossible. He looked up at her.

"Fine. I'll bury him. After I stitch up my arm," he added bitterly, heading back toward the trees and whistling sharply for Patriot, who had already been heading his way. He patted the horse as she came close. "It'll give Patriot some time to rest. We're going to walk the rest of the day, I think. She won't get the rest she needs with us riding her." Evelyn just nodded.

Jack picked up the rifle and brushed it off, checking for damage as he headed for the stream. He removed his shirt again, grumbling about having just washed it. It was his only shirt, besides his Sunday shirt, which he was going to have to dig out of the saddle bags now.

"Unsaddle Patriot," he told Evelyn over his shoulder. "Let the poor girl rest."

He didn't hear a reply, but heard the sound of Evelyn fiddling with the saddle straps. Good enough. If she tried to ride off again, he was going to shoot her, he decided. The woman was insane.

Splashing cold water over his wound, he winced. Giving it a critical eye, he nodded to himself. Just a flesh wound, and he could stitch it up just fine himself. After a few swallows of whiskey, anyway. He tried not to think what would have happened if her aim had been a bit closer to her intended target. The bullet would have gone straight through his chest.

After washing the wound, the cold water slowing the blood flow, he pressed his ruined shirt against it until he could stop the flow completely. He went to the saddlebags, which Evelyn had removed from Patriot's back as she unsaddled her. Opening the flap, he dug in until he found the small pouch with the needle and thread.

Handy for hemming both shirts and bullet wounds, he thought bitterly. He also pulled out the flask of good whiskey he kept handy. Finding a good log to sit down on, he sat and set up his supplies.

"Are you really going to stitch yourself up?" she asked, coming up beside him.

"Not the first time," he replied.

"Let me do it," she said.

"Are you kidding? A horse thief and attempted murderer?"

"I feel bad enough about all of that without you helping to make me feel more guilty," she said sharply. He almost snapped back, but saw the tears she was fighting and shut his mouth.

"Fine. You ever stitch a wound before?"

"No, but I've seen it done, and I'm a fair hand with a needle and thread. I can do it."

"Fine. I reckon you won't do a worse job than I would," he said, using his teeth to unscrew the lid of the flask before taking a long pull. He then splashed a liberal dose over the wound, hissing through his teeth as the strong liquor burned the wound.

"How many times have you been shot?" she asked as she sat down beside him and picked up the needle and thread.

"Once more than I had been yesterday," he replied sourly.

"Oh, that's a real knee-slapper," she replied dryly. He clenched his jaw as he felt the needle enter his skin.

Evelyn was surprisingly gentle. She was right, she was a fair hand with a needle. He looked over at her, so close to him and focused on his arm. He could feel the warmth of her fingers on his skin as she held his arm with one hand, the other moving with the needle.

This woman would be the death of him, he thought bitterly. Either from stressing him into an early grave, or maybe by accidentally shooting him again. It could go either way, at this point.

"Four," he said after several minutes.

"What?"

"This makes four times I've been shot. Once with a six-shooter, here," he said as he pointed out the scar near his shoulder. It had gone clean through, and he pointed at the exit scar on his back as well. "Once caught a few pellets from a scattergun here," he added, pointing at the three small, round scars on one side of his stomach, near his side. "And now twice with a long rifle."

Jack tapped the other scar, along one side of his neck. It was a subtle scar, and probably hadn't been deep. It was a longer scar, a grazing blow like the one she'd just given him, though that one had been much closer to killing him. Some days, he wished it had.

"Did those happen when you rode with the Saints of Laredo?" she asked as she worked another stitch.

"Two did. The other was before, when I rode with a less pleasant crowd."

"You rode with a different group before the Saints? Doing what?" she asked curiously. Here she goes again, he thought. And despite himself, he told her.

"Less pleasant men doing less pleasant things. I was… angry. With the world, I suppose. Wanted to take some of that out on other people. Took a while before my brothers in the Saints turned me around." She was quiet for another minute before speaking again.

"Why were you so angry?" she asked, softly.

He didn't respond right away, thoughts of Lucy and the children setting his eyes burning. He hadn't thought of them so much in a lot of years, and certainly not enough for him to get emotional about it. Jack had closed that part of himself away long ago. Why it was suddenly coming back up, he had no idea.

"You about done?" he asked gruffly, taking

another swallow of the whiskey.

"Just about," she replied with a sigh. She finished in silence.

When she was done, he looked down at the work, and nodded approvingly.

"Far cry better than I'd have done. Thank you," he added.

"It's the least I could do, since I'm the one who shot you."

"Seems fair. All right, now I'm going to tie you up."

"What?" she asked in shock, leaning back.

"You've proven more than once that you can't be trusted. I've got a job to do, and you've gotten a lot of people, myself included, hurt with your nonsense. We're taking the rest of this ride my way."

She opened her mouth to protest, but shut it quickly. Looking down, she nodded, and held her hands out to him, wrists together. He stood and moved to get the rope. She didn't resist as he tied first her hands, then her ankles. He adjusted her position to the ground, to make sure she'd be comfortable. He then tied her ankles on a six-foot length of rope to one of his own. She frowned, but didn't protest.

"Now, we're going to let Patriot, and myself, get a little shut-eye. We'll head out again in a few hours and move until nightfall. We'll camp for the night, and get a full day's ride in tomorrow. I hear anything out of your mouth I don't like, and I'm gagging you again. Am I clear?"

Again, she looked like she was going to protest, but she didn't. He gave her a few swallows of water, and put the flask of whiskey away, taking a long pull of the canteen himself before refilling it from the stream. It was at the extent of his tether to her, but he had made sure to give enough lead rope to let him reach the water.

He then lay down on the saddle blanket, adjusted the position of the gun in the back of the belt and closed his eyes, hand resting carefully near the gun at his hip.

Jack couldn't decide if he wanted to thrash the woman, or kiss her. He needed to keep her bound, and probably gagged, to make sure he didn't do either. This was going to be one of the longest bounty runs of his life, and he'd chased down men as far away as Nevada, and with a heap less trouble the whole ride than he'd had in one day with this woman.

Jack took a long breath to calm himself and tried to sleep. He didn't think he'd be able to, but at least he had to try. He needed to be as sharp as possible to deal with whatever trouble she brought him next.

If ever Jack had been sure of anything in his life, it was that one way or another, this wasn't the last of the trouble she'd bring his way.

Chapter Six

Evie felt more guilty than she ever had in her entire life. They'd been back on the road for a couple of hours, and neither of them had said a word. True to his word, he'd kept her tied up. She couldn't really blame him. He had not, however, gagged her, and had also not slung her over the back of his horse, though she felt she deserved both. She was infinitely grateful he hadn't, though.

She rode astride Patriot, despite his saying they'd walk the rest of the day. Her hands were bound to the saddle horn, another length of rope running from her ankle to his wrist as he walked beside her. Jack had told her if she tried to bolt on the horse, he'd shoot her before the rope could go taut. Evie wasn't entirely sure that he was joking.

The ruined shirt had been torn into strips to use for bandaging, and he now wore his Sunday shirt, which she desperately hoped he wouldn't bleed through. The shirt was a sage green, and the fabric looked as smooth as the color. She could see why his friend had called it a Sunday shirt. It wouldn't have been out of place in a church at all, though Jack wearing a shirt that nice seemed more than a little out of place.

Not that she didn't think Jack could look nice and fancy like that, just that right now he looked a bit haggard. He hadn't shaved since at least the day before, had a light sheen of road dust covering his jeans and hat, though he'd washed his face and hands in the creek before they'd set out again. He also looked like a man at the end of his rope, both literally and figuratively.

He was right. A lot of people had gotten hurt because of her stunt back in town, and he'd been shot himself and left a man dead back by the creek. It was all her fault, whatever he said.

Her father may have been the one to put the bounty out for her, but he only had to do it because she'd disobeyed him and run off with Frank, who, just as her father said he would, had jumped into another woman's arms at the first opportunity. It brought up the uncomfortable possibility that he may have been right about more things, as well. How embarrassing that would be!

Her own stubbornness had left her on her own in Nebraska, struggling to survive in a country that was famous for killing people who weren't both careful and lucky. She'd survived, but now this had happened. Maybe she should have listened to her father and stayed in Topeka, marrying whatever political ally he'd decided on for her, to strengthen his own position.

No, she snapped at herself. That last was precisely why she shouldn't have stayed. Whatever had happened since leaving, she was nobody's property to be traded for political favors, money, or anything else. She deserved the right to marry whomever she wished, whenever she wished. She deserved to marry for love, despite her father insisting there was no such thing.

Evie knew there was, though. She'd seen the way her mother had loved her father before she'd been killed. He obviously didn't feel the same, which put an unpleasant kink in Evie's faith in the concept. She knew it existed, but had never seen it go both ways. She believed it could, was absolutely certain. But she'd never seen it. If it didn't, what was the point of love at all? It couldn't be just to bring good women into the hands of unpleasant men.

It was part of why she'd never pursued anyone else in the five years since Frank. She'd been so sure she was in love with him. He didn't love her, though. He'd made that quite clear. And she'd gotten over him much faster than she thought real love should be recovered from.

She'd needed him, she knew. That was all. If only to get out of Topeka. Once that had been done and he'd proven unfaithful, it had taken only days for her to dry her eyes, cowgirl up, and get to work.

Evie remembered her mother, though. It had been twelve years since she'd been killed, but the love she'd shown both to Evie's father and to Evie herself had always resonated in her thoughts. It had to be possible for that to go both ways.

Lord knew there were countless songs about one-sided love, and only a handful of real love, felt by both. Poems, art, music, all seemed to portray far more cases of the unrequited than of soulmates.

It didn't matter, she reminded herself. Whether it existed or not, she didn't have it, and never would, if she did as her father wished. She needed to find a way to escape again.

And get more people hurt, she thought? She almost shouted in frustration. Evie looked down at Jack where he walked beside Patriot. He was walking in stony silence, his rugged features set in an expression of grim determination. She looked away, another pang of guilt stabbing her in the gut.

The sun was setting to her right, casting its beautiful orange and crimson hues out across the grassland. The few small trees were casting long shadows toward her, and the sound of the night animals had begun, the yip of a fox or the hoot of an owl punctuating the clip-clop of Patriot's hoofbeats.

Evie knew she shouldn't feel guilty. Two bounty hunters had gotten into a gunfight trying to determine which was going to continue her abduction and unwilling return to a man who planned to literally sell her off for his own gain. Like most guilt, however, it didn't respond to rationalization or reason.

"We're going to stop right over there," Jack said, interrupting her brooding. He was pointing to a fairly large tree quite a distance from the road.

Evie nodded, still not sure what to say to him. They made it to the tree, and he reached up to help her down. He took Patriot's saddle and saddlebags off, and began his brushing ritual with her after giving her another apple.

He didn't tie her legs, so Evie began wandering around, collecting firewood and hunting for good firepit stones, though the latter she had to roll with her bound hands.

The grass was sparse under the broad reach of the tree, and the branches were high enough that there wasn't any real worry of problems with a small fire here. She'd finished awkwardly rolling the firepit stones over, and had begun working on preparing for the fire when he came over.

"Thanks," he said simply. She nodded and stepped back, letting him lean down to finish the fire. He reached down to make adjustments, then paused and considered a moment before nodding, not changing a thing. "Good build," he said.

"Thank you," she replied.

Evie didn't have much experience building a fire, but she'd watched him closely when he'd built the ones for breakfast and lunch. Closer than she should have, probably.

Bringing flint and steel out of his pocket, he

began working on getting the fire started. She moved back and sat down, leaning back against the big trunk of the tree, watching him again.

Whatever closeness she'd been building with him was gone. He'd been all iron and ice since she'd run off with Patriot. It had been stupid, and she knew it. She hadn't even had a plan beyond getting away.

With the fire going, he began cooking. He cooked and they ate in silence. Jack had made some kind of biscuits to go with the beans he cooked over the fire in a small pot, and produced a small jar of honey to go with them.

She was once again struck by how well he managed to cook out in the middle of nowhere. The biscuits were delicious. He even seasoned up the beans and they were the best she'd ever had.

After eating, he'd set out his bedroll, and gestured her into it. As she climbed in, wondering where he was going to sleep, he roped her ankles again, tying the six-foot lead to his own ankle. He gave her a slightly apologetic look as he did so, but that was all he offered.

She would take it, and gratefully. He was even giving up his own bedroll for her, she couldn't ask for more. He lay down on the saddle blanket, not quite to the extent of the lead rope, tucking his hat down low over his eyes, arms folded back behind his head.

Evie watched him for several minutes, conflict

growing in her mind. She didn't want to go back to Topeka. But would it be so terrible if she did? She'd see her father again, he could remind her why she had left in the first place, and she would leave again.

If she cooperated, they'd get there sooner and Jack could collect his pay and move along. She had very mixed feelings about that, but it was what was best for Jack. And very probably for her, as well.

Of course, her father would likely have security posted on her night and day once she got back, so it would be much harder to escape a second time. He was also likely to push hard to marry her off quickly, and wouldn't be likely to ease off his watch on her until the knot had been tied.

It was probably easier to escape one man, Jack, than the unknown number of private security forces her father hired. He would probably even have the law keeping an eye out for her. She looked at Jack again. He was breathing deeply and softly.

In the distance, a coyote howled. She sat up, suddenly nervous.

"Nothing to be scared of, darlin'," Jack said from under his hat. He hadn't moved. "Just the coyotes singing to each other."

"Aren't they dangerous?"

"Can be, but not out here. The three of us are too much for a handful of coyotes to want to tangle with. Besides, there's plenty of game out here, so they sure ain't starving. That's a friendly song, anyway."

"A friendly song?"

Jack sat up, tipping his hat back. He listened to another pair of coyotes answering the first.

"Sure is. You hear that? The first one called out a howdy to his friends, and the other two are answering back, telling him where they are. I reckon they'll be joining up soon to do a bit of rollicking in the grass, maybe hunt some gophers." They listened for a while as the animals howled again before going silent.

"How do you know what they're saying?" she asked softly in wonder.

"Spend enough nights alone out here, and you start to get real friendly with the locals. Can you reach the saddlebag? There's a harmonica in a little box in there. Toss that over, would you?"

Curious, she reached out and got hold of the bag, fishing through until she found the small, worn box. She tossed it to Jack, who caught it smoothly. He opened the box and brought out an old, even more worn harmonica.

Evie watched in fascination as he put the small instrument to his lips. Instead of music, like she expected, he sounded a long, lonely note that arced high in pitch before dropping down low before tapering off.

He lowered the harmonica and listened. Evie listened as well. Only a few moments later, all three coyotes howled back. Jack smiled.

"You see?" he said, turning the smile her way.

"That's… amazing," she said. He chuckled that deep sound she was quickly growing to love.

"I just told them we needed a song. They're going to sing us to sleep," he seemed to suddenly realize who he was smiling at, and the smile slipped.

Their eyes stayed locked together for a long moment, the coyotes howling a peculiar, but oddly comforting melody in the distance before Jack suddenly looked away, laying back down.

"Goodnight, Evelyn," he said softly.

She almost started at the sound of her name. He'd been calling her "ma'am" and "darlin'," all day. This was the first time he'd ever used her name, and all she could think was that she desperately wished he'd called her Evie instead. She wanted to tell him to call her that, but it wasn't right.

She lay back and listened to the coyotes sing, mind wandering. In likely two days time, she'd be back at her old childhood home, staring her father in the eyes for the first time in five years. Jack would collect his reward and be on his way. She'd be in a different predicament altogether, and he'd be… wherever he decided to go after unloading her.

For the hundredth time, she caught herself wishing she'd met Jack under nearly any other circumstances. Reaching over, she moved to close the saddlebag but caught sight of something that drew her eyes.

It was a piece of folded paper. Thinking it might be her bounty contract, she pulled it out and carefully unfolded it. Glancing at Jack's still form, she looked back at the paper. What she saw hit her like a punch in the gut.

The paper wasn't a contract. On it was drawn a picture in charcoal, in the obvious hand of a young child. The picture showed a small house next to a field of corn. In front of the house were four figures; a man in a wide-brimmed hat, a woman with long hair, a girl about half the height of the adults, and what might possibly have been a baby in a small cradle.

At the top of the page, just under a blocky sun, was written in the same child's scrawl "Fur pa". It took her only a moment to realize that the message was a dedication to the child's father. The picture was probably a gift. Why did Jack have this? Was he the pa in this picture? If he was, what had happened?

She had to admit from what she knew about Jack that it was possible this picture had been taken from someone Jack might even have killed. Maybe this was the incident that had turned him from his gang, and set him out to riding with the Saints.

In either case, she knew without a doubt this was the reason he always sounded a little sad when he talked about his past. Whomever this family was, they meant something to him.

She carefully folded the paper and put it back in the saddlebag, closing the flap. She lay back down, and looked again over at Jack. His breathing was still steady and slow. She wiped an errant tear from an eye she hadn't realized had begun to water, and rolled over. Evie knew she wouldn't sleep tonight.

Jack gently shook Evie awake. She stirred slowly, having been sleeping quite comfortably. She locked eyes with him as they opened, and she frowned a question at him. He gave a slight shake of his head.

As she opened her mouth to ask what was going on, he put a finger to his lips. She nodded, but looked concerned. The sky had just begun to brighten at the horizon, and dawn was likely still some time off.

He finished untying her, and began quickly saddling Patriot. His steady hand and whispered words kept the horse calm and quiet, but he could tell Evie was agitated.

She came close and leaned in, whispering her question. Jack pointedly ignored the way his body almost instinctively leaned in to meet hers.

"What is it?"

Leaning right down by her ear, he answered in a voice so soft it wouldn't have carried more than a few inches.

"Indians," he replied. "Scouting party. We need to go before they come down this way."

Eyes wide, she nodded, quickly and quietly

rolling up the bedroll and helping him get the saddlebags. Mounting quickly, he reached down and helped her mount up behind him. She reached out and held onto him as he silently nudged Patriot forward.

They rode quietly until the sun began to crest the horizon. Only then did either of them speak. Evelyn's voice barely above a whisper.

"What was that about?"

"Tsawi scouting party," he replied, voice still soft, but not too cautious, which made her relax a little against him. He pushed away the thought of how nice it felt, having her riding behind him, arms around his waist. "They're not naturally hostile, but there are a lot of resentments with the white folk for running them off their lands. Maybe wouldn't go over well if they came across the two of us in their territory. I could probably talk us out of it, but better to play our cards a mite closer than that."

"Why are we in Indian territory?" she asked, sounding concerned.

"It was all Indian territory, until we came and stole it. They've got every right to be angry with us. But to your real question, we need to stay off the major roadways. That's where your father's enemies would be most likely to catch us. Means we won't see much civilization, though, and we'll be crossing through more Indian territory than not."

"You don't sound afraid of them. More like you feel bad for them," she pointed out.

"I do. They've been treated more unfairly than any other folk I know. An old friend of mine is Crow. Or half, anyway."

"You're friends with Indians?" she asked, surprised.

"Just him. One of the Saints," he clarified. He wasn't sure why he was letting his guard down with her again, but there it was.

"How many of you were there?"

"Six," Jack answered. He found he really wanted to tell her, which surprised him. He hadn't talked about the Saints in years. "All but Grady used to ride with the same gang of outlaws I did. We all left together. Storm-Chaser was our tracker. Jarrett was the fastest gun I've ever seen. Santiago could pick a flea off a horse's back with a long rifle at five hundred yards, and put a man's eye out at near a thousand. We kept Lucky around mostly for fun. He was as likely to shoot his own foot off as hit the target. He sure could drink, though, and he did love a good card game."

Jack was smiling again. He couldn't remember the last time he'd smiled so much. The woman had nearly gotten him killed more than once, but she still brought his smile out with alarming regularity.

It was sad, thinking about his brothers again, but not as sharp as it used to be. His regrets were still just as strong, however. He hoped they were all well in whatever lives they'd chosen to pursue.

"What about, what was it, Grady?" she asked.

Jack chuckled at the name.

"Kid Grady was a smooth talker. Pretty handy with a gun, but it was mostly trick shots. We rescued him from an Apache raiding party about five seconds before they scalped him. Never could get rid of the runt after that."

"How old was he?"

"Oh, maybe nineteen at the time. The boy stuck to us like glue. We taught him how to not get his fool self killed, and he made himself useful in a fight more than once."

"Kind of you all to take him in," she said.

"Kind nothing. We spent six months trying to shake him. Finally gave up and took the kid in because it was easier than trying to get rid of him. Good lad, though. Carried his weight, once he got a little less wet behind the ears."

"So what happened?" she asked.

Jack felt himself starting to wall up again, but something about the compassion in her tone, and his inexplicable, sudden need to share with her, got him to let her in just a little more.

"Grady got stupid. Roped us all into a pretty big mess. There was a lot of fighting among the Saints over it, and we all decided to go our separate ways before someone got shot."

"Would it have come to that?" Evelyn asked.

"I don't reckon so. They would, and did, split before anyone got riled enough to draw iron."

"Where did everyone go?"

"Can't say, for sure." Jack honestly didn't know, but had heard a few things here and there. "I think Santiago started farming. He always wanted to. Said it's what his ma would have wanted for him. Lucky got into playing professional poker tournaments, but I'm not sure how he fared. That was some time ago. Jarrett found Jesus, as they say. I think he's preaching in some one-horse town somewhere in the Dakotas. Haven't heard anything about Storm-Chaser or Grady since the split. I reckon Kid Grady's probably gotten himself killed by now, without us around. He never did know when to keep his mouth shut. Storm-Chaser, who knows? Maybe he went back to the Crow."

"Did you ever try to get back together with them?" she asked. He hesitated.

"I talked to Jarrett once, a few months after. He kept trying to get me to come to church with him, thought sure I'd find my answers there like he did. He'll never ride again. The Saints of Laredo won't ever ride again."

"I'm sorry," she said, sincerely.

He nodded, appreciating the sentiment. It was a good time in his life. The best since before he'd ridden with the gang. It was a time when he'd felt like he was helping people, saving lives, making amends for some of the damage he'd done, if only one little step at a time.

Jack took a long breath. It felt good to talk about his brothers again, even if they were no longer his brothers.

No, he corrected, they would always be his brothers. They were bonded by more than blood. Even a split like they'd had wouldn't stop him riding hard to give his life for any one of them if the occasion called for it. He couldn't say if they all felt the same, but it didn't change his thoughts on the matter one whit.

"Wagon train ahead. We should go around," Jack said, as he spotted a small caravan of three wagons as the dawn light began to spill into a little valley below.

"Wait," Evelyn said, pointing. "Look at that. I think they might need help, Mr. Hannity."

"Jack," he corrected automatically.

"We're not that friendly," she replied. He could hear the smile in her voice and smiled, too.

Jack's eyes followed where she pointed and he saw what she meant. The floor of the small valley had gathered some water from the last rainfall four days ago, and the trail the wagons had been following had turned muddy enough that it was still pretty thick.

The front wagon was well and truly stuck. He watched a moment as they tried to pull the wagon loose, but it wasn't budging. The men were trying to simply forge straight ahead, forcing the wheels deeper into the mud. If they turned the oxen sharply to one side or another, only a few feet would get them onto the less-muddy slope. Trying to plow directly through would have them stuck there forever.

"They'll get it," he said, starting to turn Patriot to swing around them.

"What if they don't? What if the Tsawi find them first? They have children down there!" she protested.

Jack watched the older children scrambling in the mud, trying to help, and could hear the youngest wailing even from here. He took a deep breath and let it out slowly.

"Not our trouble, Miss Delano," he said, though even he could hear there wasn't much conviction in it.

She had a point. They'd be a lot less likely to talk their way out of trouble if the Tsawi found them out here than he could. Besides, he could tell from the way they were working down below that they were going about the problem in entirely the wrong way, and were likely to be there all day. Maybe longer.

"We have to help," she said, insistently. He sighed and nodded.

"All right, but we're gone the moment they're free. And you behave yourself, Miss Delano. This isn't the time or place to cause trouble, these are innocent folk."

"I will," she said, so sincerely and contritely that he looked back to see if she was mocking him. He was momentarily touched when he saw that she wasn't. Maybe she'd learned her lesson after all, he thought.

Probably not, he thought with a sigh, nudging Patriot down the hill toward the ruckus below.

Chapter Seven

The two men by the wagons below saw them coming and scrambled for their rifles. Evie slid down tighter behind Jack, but he calmly held up one hand peacefully in greeting, and the men eased, but only just, and not without getting the rifles in hand first.

"Mornin'!" Jack called as they neared. The women had rounded up the children and were huddling them behind one of the wagons. The two men stood ready, rifles not aimed at Jack and Evie, but ready to come up fast if they felt threatened.

"Morning," one of the men said cautiously.

"Stand easy, sir, we mean no harm," Jack said. Evie leaned out around him, making herself visible. She waved to the group of women and children as well.

"We're just coming down to lend a hand, if you'll have it," Evie said.

The entire group relaxed at her manner and appearance. She smiled to herself. Jack was a little intimidating, she had to admit. She dismounted with a hand from Jack. He followed suit a moment later, and let her lead their walk up to the two men.

"Looks like you've gotten yourselves a mite bogged down," she said with a friendly smile.

"That we have. We aren't looking for trouble, just trying to make it to Kansas City."

"Got a ways to go," Jack said, nodding. "Four, maybe five days with those oxen setting the pace. Not a bad journey, though. Easy trails if you can get to a major one."

"We just need to get ourselves unstuck, and we can be on our way."

Evie nodded, as friendly as she could make herself appear. These families were skittish, she thought. She wondered if they'd had trouble already. Neither of these men looked the trail type. One looked like a bookkeeper and the other might have been a craftsman of some sort. Neither looked like they'd been more than a few miles outside of town their whole lives.

"I can help with that," Jack said, setting down Patriot's reins and tapping them with a foot. She'd seen him do that before and knew Patriot wouldn't move until someone picked up her reigns again.

"Come along, then," the bigger man said, gesturing.

Jack took off his coat, and the smaller man visibly flinched as he saw Jack's gun. However, Jack just removed the gun belt and put it across Patriot's back, moving to follow the big man. The smaller man followed them to the front wagon. Evie moved to the women and children. She smiled and waved again.

"Good morning," she said.

"Good morning," came the reply from the oldest of the three women. She was a good deal older than the other two.

"Lucky we came along. Could have been out here all day," Evie said. "Don't worry, Jack will get it sorted. He's handy as they come. My name's Evie."

"Mighty glad to hear that," the older woman said. "My boys aren't really range riders, but they've got jobs in Kansas City, and want a better life for their families. My name's Ethel, and these are my daughters-in-law, Maryanne and Ida."

Evie nodded in greeting to each as they were introduced.

"Pleasure," Evie said. "We're just heading down to Topeka, ourselves. Going to live with my father for a while."

She turned her head to check on Jack. He was obviously trying to explain something, and the two men weren't getting it. He looked unflustered, though, which made her smile. She was starting to wonder if she was the only person who ever agitated him. For some reason, that thought warmed her.

"Well, we were about to stop for breakfast," Maryanne said. "We've been traveling nights to avoid the Indians. Heard that was safest. Wanted to make it a bit further first, but it'll take them some time to get the wagon free. Would you like to help us get some breakfast made for the boys?"

"I'd be happy to," she said. As the women bustled around gathering ingredients and getting a small cooking fire going, Evie watched the children play.

They ran and laughed, wrestling and shoving. It was the kind of horseplay she'd seen neighbor children enjoy, but that she, as the daughter of a distinguished member of the upper class, had never been permitted. She was an only child, too, so she didn't even have siblings to horse around with, even had it been allowed.

She listened to them playing, and chatted idly with the three women, all the while marveling at the realization that this was what she wanted. Not the wagon train, no thank you, but a family. She wanted a husband who would do his best to care for her, like these poor men were trying so hard to do, and a couple of small children playing in the yard.

As she began to envision this lifestyle, she suddenly realized that the man who kept appearing in the role as her husband was Jack. It was ridiculous, she knew. A man like Jack would never settle down, least of all with her. She couldn't even imagine him with children. Except that she could, and it was beautiful.

He was fair but firm, playful but tough. She could see him laughing as he tossed a child into the air, and could see him cowing a roomful of rowdy youngsters with that icy tone and his hawklike gaze.

Perhaps he had been a father, she realized as she remembered the drawing she'd found in his bags the night before. Maybe he'd done all those things before… before whatever had happened.

If that life had ended in tragedy, he'd likely never want to put himself in that position again. But maybe he hadn't been a father, she reminded herself. It was unpleasantly possible that he'd been responsible for something that had happened to the family in the picture, and it was his regret about that action that drove him to a dangerous, reclusive lifestyle.

Whatever it was, a man like Jack didn't settle down. He'd ride the range until the day he died, which wouldn't likely take too long before someone got the better of him.

Jack had nearly died just yesterday, she thought. Twice, since Hound could have killed him, or she could, with as far off as her aim had been. The thought that she might have killed him herself made her a mite nauseated.

Evie's thoughts were interrupted once more by the sound of excited shouts from the men as the redirected oxen successfully pulled the wagon wheels free and onto the firm hill slope. The children all cheered as well, and the women gave a whoop. Evie cheered herself, caught up in the moment with this kind, gentle family.

"You must stay and eat with us. It's the least we can do for your help," Ethel insisted.

"Oh, we don't want to impose. We really should get going," Evie said reluctantly.

"Don't go listening to none of that nonsense," Jack said with a smile as he came over with the other two men. "We'd be proud to eat with you and yours. Fine pair of menfolk you've got here. Can't help but admire their determination."

"We couldn't have done it without you," the bigger man said, clapping Jack on the shoulder. Jack smiled.

"You'd have managed, I've no doubt."

"Well, come on over and get some chow then, boys," Ida called to the men.

As the men were served up some of the potatoes and bacon, Evie couldn't seem to pull her eyes from Jack. He was talking and laughing, chatting in the friendliest way. He seemed like the kind of man you'd see at any get-together. Just a friendly neighbor having a good time. It sent her earlier thoughts about him in the role of husband and father into another swirling deluge of fantasies.

He turned and looked at her, laughing at something one of the men said, and the smile on his face sent her whole heart thudding in her chest.

She could argue the circumstances all she wanted, but she could no longer argue that this is what she wanted. And she wanted it with him.

Turning away, she bit back a pang of regret. She

knew it wasn't possible. Even if everything else were different, he wouldn't want her.

"Come eat, darlin'!" she heard him call. Turning back to face him, she put a smile on her face and came over to the group.

Taking a bowl of food, she went and sat across from him near the fire. He'd sat himself atop a small crate, where he seemed to be relishing the food. She absently took a bite and nearly choked.

Good Lord, what did those women do to these poor, unsuspecting potatoes! She cast a dubious look into the bowl. She'd only had a few meals made by Jack, but already her palate seemed to have shifted to a richer spectrum, expecting more from trail food. These potatoes weren't bland, they were bitter, and slightly sour, neither being flavors she ever attributed to the poor tuber.

Evie looked back up to Jack, who was watching her with what seemed a perfectly innocent smile, but his eyes were dancing. He'd been waiting to see how she reacted to the food, she realized. Jack took another bite, pretending to enjoy it immensely, casting a wink her way.

She couldn't help but smile as she forced herself to take another bite. She chewed and swallowed with some difficulty, and he laughed at something one of the men said, but she felt sure he was really laughing at her.

One of the children, a boy about seven or eight, was sneaking up behind Jack. He didn't seem to notice as he chatted with the smaller of the two men. In a sudden burst, the boy charged him, leaping toward him. Jack spun on one heel, leaning forward off the box, arm snaking out and grabbing the boy in mid-leap. With a snarl, Jack swung the boy high and wide, drawing a shout of excitement from the lad. Bringing the boy back down to the ground, he set the lad down.

"Attacking from behind, you yellow varmint? Let's see if you can face me like a man!" Jack growled at the child.

The boy gave a whoop and ran back several steps, snatching up a nearby stick and turning back to face Jack.

"You think that'll save you?" Jack asked, taking a slow, even step toward the boy, who laughed delightedly.

The boy lunged with the stick, and Jack snatched it out of his hand as quick as a striking viper. Tossing it aside, he moved quickly toward the boy, who was yelling in mock terror. Out of nowhere, three other small children charged Jack, leaping at his legs, clinging to his arms, clawing at his back.

Jack laughed in surprise as the children wrestled him willingly to the ground. The whole mess of children, Jack, and the children's families were all laughing, the parents cheering the children on.

Evie was captivated. Here he was, behaving exactly like she'd envisioned in her daydreams. With sudden, absolute conviction, she knew; the family in the beautifully innocent child's drawing had been his.

She gathered Jack's dishes and her own, and went to help the women with the cleanup. All the while, she watched Jack playing with the children. The other men had joined in, and it had turned into a children versus men all-out brawl. There were cowboy hollers and Indian whoops, but nobody appeared certain which side was which. Nobody seemed to much care, either.

"He's a good man," Ethel said to her. Evie looked over to see the older woman eyeing her closely.

"He is," Evie agreed.

"You shouldn't let that one get away," Ethel added.

"Pardon?" Evie asked, not wanting to admit that she knew exactly what the elderly matron of the family had meant.

"Evie, honey, I don't know what the situation is between you two. I truly don't. But what I do know is that you're looking at him like a lost lamb who's finally spotted home."

Evie blushed deeply, embarrassed that she'd been so obvious.

"It's not... it isn't like that," she tried to argue.

"Now, child, I don't know much, but I know love when I see it." At this, Evie's surprise showed plainly on her face.

"Love? Now, Ethel, I think you're reading a mite too far into this. I've only known him…"

"I most certainly am not," the old woman interrupted. "As I said, I know love when I see it."

"It's ridiculous," Evie argued. "It can't work that way. He's… no, it just can't. Circumstances would get in the way even if he wanted me, which he doesn't."

"Oh, I wouldn't go betting my last dollar on that wager, honey."

"What? Why do you say that?"

"I can see the way he looks at you, too."

"What do you mean?"

"Look at him, Evie. Real quick, just look."

Evie turned her eyes to Jack, who was standing to one side, breathing hard, hands on his hips as he tried to catch his breath with a smile on his face, and looking at her. His smile broadened slightly as he met her gaze.

"See that, now? That smile was for you. Nobody else. Just you."

"Ethel, I think you might just be a touch mad," Evie protested, the color in her cheeks deepening.

"Oh, I've no doubt," laughed the woman, "but the fact remains, he sees something in you, too. Something that makes him smile like that. As I said, he's a good man, a fine looker, too. Helping folk, and rollicking with the children and such. A whole passel of women would trade just about everything for what you've got standing right in front of you."

"He's just… not the settling down type. And circumstances… I wish I could explain. It just can't work," Evie said, looking down at the half-washed dish in her hands.

"Well, you do what you like, honey. I don't know you from Eve, I just know what I see. And what I see is a lifetime of regret if you let that buck get away. Just think about it, now."

Evie nodded, unsure what else to say. A day and a half with Jack and she felt like her entire world had changed. Who she was, what she wanted, how she felt, all of it had been turned upside down by a man whose sole purpose was to give her back to a man who intended to sell her off like cattle.

Ethel didn't understand. Jack didn't look at her like that. He couldn't. All he could see was the bounty, and keeping her roped in so she didn't get away.

Whether she loved him or not, and Ethel's words had made her realize that she was indeed falling for Jack, and hard, it made no difference. In the end, he would hand her over to her father. At this point, she should just be grateful he wasn't trying to take advantage of her in any way. She thought of Hound and shuddered.

Not long after, they bid their goodbyes to the family.

"Keep heading east," Jack was saying, "and you'll reach a fork in this trail. Take the south fork. It'll cost you about two hours more trail time before you reach the main road to Kansas City, but the north trail had a Tsawi scouting patrol running it not long ago. Southern trail will be safer. You can reach the main road in about six or seven hours, once you leave from here."

"Thank you, Jack," the big man said, reaching out to shake Jack's hand. The younger man shook his hand as well.

"Couldn't have done it without you. That was a real kindness, and no mistake. You take care of that little filly," he said, tipping his hat to Evie, who blushed.

"Believe me, I aim to," Jack said with a chuckle. Evie's smile slipped, since she knew what he really meant by that.

The women and children called their goodbyes again as Evie and Jack rode south away from the beautiful family.

"That was real sweet of you," Evie said softly.

"You're the one who insisted we stop and help," he argued.

"I meant pretending the food wasn't absolutely terrible," she said. Jack looked back at her in surprise, then burst into laughter.

"I'd have warned you," he got out after a moment to catch his breath, "but watching you take that first bite was too much!" She laughed, too.

"Thank you for that. You're a real gentleman," she replied sardonically.

"Only as much as I can get away with," he

retorted. "So… Evie?"

She blushed again. He'd heard the family calling her that all morning. She hadn't realized he'd never heard it before, but where would he have heard it? Certainly not from her father. Her father refused to call her anything but Evelyn. He said nicknames were unsophisticated.

"My friends call me Evie," she explained.

"So I should call you Miss Delano?" he asked, looking back over his shoulder again, that light dancing in his eyes again.

"You certainly should," she replied, tone playfully stern. He chuckled.

"You did good back there," he told her. "I'm glad you didn't try to cause trouble. That was a good family, and I'm grateful we got to be friendly and then leave them peacefully. I don't often get to interact with folk like that."

"Peacefully?" she asked. He grinned at her over his shoulder.

"I actually meant casually, but peacefully suits, too. I only really deal with folk for business, so it was a nice change to spend some time being around real people for a spell."

They rode in silence for a long while before either of them spoke again.

"What happened to them?" she asked.

"To who?" he replied.

"I saw the picture, in your saddlebags," she admitted. His body tensed, and he didn't respond.

"I wasn't snooping, you've got my word on that. I saw it when I was reaching for your harmonica, and thought it was my bounty contract. I didn't mean to nose in."

He was quiet long enough that she wondered if he were angry with her. She watched the clouds drifting across the wide open sky. There was a gentle breeze, just enough to keep things cool and make the long grass shimmer in rippling waves.

In moments like this, Evie could readily see how Jack spent so much of his time comfortably alone out here. Here was where he found the divine, she remembered fondly.

"It's all right, I believe you. I didn't exactly have it hidden. Most times, I'm not likely to let a bounty go rooting around in my bags, so I was never too worried about what they might see."

"You don't have to explain, I just… it looked like something that meant a lot. I wanted to know that about you."

"Plan to try and use it against me to escape?" he asked. She wasn't sure if he were joking, but it didn't matter. The message was clear.

"No," she answered honestly. "I just wanted to understand you a little better."

"That's fair. Well, it's no secret. There was a newspaper article on it and everything, though that was a long time ago. I just don't much talk about it these days. Or much of anything else, really."

"You seem to talk to me just fine," she pointed

out.

"Yeah," he agreed, looking suspiciously back at her. "How exactly do you do that?" She laughed softly.

"I wish I knew, truly."

"Well," he continued, "remember I told you that sometimes the law takes too long, and folks sometimes get hurt while waiting for the paperwork?"

"I do."

"My family were some of those folks. I married young. It was right, though. I loved her, more than anything. She loved me too, more's the miracle. Raised a small herd of cattle on a small ranch. Had two little ones, too. My daughter was learning her letters. Her ma made her practice writing her letters on those drawings she was always doing. I usually made her use bark for them, but her mother let her use a piece of real paper for that one, as a present. The stuff ain't cheap, but it was well worth it. Wrote that out all by herself. I couldn't have been prouder. Anyway, our boy was still just a little one."

Evie sat still and quiet, afraid to disturb him. He was going to tell her all of it. She was stunned he'd opened up again. She really wished she did know how she did that to him.

Jack's voice had slipped into that sadness she'd heard before, and the regret in it made her heart ache for him. Her throat constricted as she anticipated what was coming next. She could hear the pain in his voice, and his pain tore into her like it was her own.

"Couple of cattle rustlers came through one day, while I'd taken the wagon into town for a few things. My wife caught them trying to make off with our herd, and took a shot at one. Killed him, too. Fine woman, she was. Brave, beautiful, and sharp as a whip."

He paused and took a long breath. Evie held hers, as much to keep from letting the tears come as anything else.

"The other one put one right in her belly," he said after a moment to collect. "Takes a long time to die from a gut wound. I've seen it happen a few times. Not a pretty way to go. She was probably still alive when they lit our house on fire. I doubt they knew or cared that our children were still in there. Made off with the whole herd. I came home late that night. There was nothing left, by then. Just soot and smoke."

Evie was trying to surreptitiously wipe the tears from her eyes, her throat so tight she was having to work hard to keep her breathing steady. His voice had gone flat and dead.

"I found that picture folded neatly and resting on the rail in the barn, next to my saddle. It had been left there to surprise me. Packed it in my saddlebags. It was literally all I had. I picked up the rifle from my wife's hands where she lay in the road, and took the gunbelt from the man she'd killed. After burying her, I mounted my horse, and rode out hard for the sheriff." He paused again. Evie couldn't even imagine the horror he'd witnessed. Nobody should have to live through something like that, she thought tearfully.

"After a week, the sheriff still hadn't made a move. Said he was waiting on approval from the state to round up a posse. Takes a special permit, apparently. I gave up waiting. Took me twelve days to find the other man. He'd already offloaded the cattle, of course. Lord only knew where the money had gone."

Evie's tears were flowing freely now. She couldn't even begin to imagine the sickening sorrow, the loss, he'd endured in those moments, and the years after.

"Caught up with him in the middle of the night while he slept. Kicked his gun away and tossed mine. I let him get up and try to fight me. I beat him to death with my bare hands. Found out later both men had been wanted in four states. But because the law had to deal with jurisdiction issues and permits and such, and the feds weren't interested in dealing with it since they were 'small time', nobody had been able to arrest them yet. Who knows how many good folk were killed because the law was too busy worrying about paperwork and bureaucracy to stop them. Didn't much care for the law after that."

"Oh, Jack, I'm so sorry," Evie got out, reaching a hand up to squeeze his shoulder comfortingly. He just nodded.

"It's been a long time, but thank you."

It all made sense to her now. He'd been a good-hearted, innocent man, with a wife, children, and his own ranch, even if it was a small one. Two men, slipping through delays in the law, had taken it all from him in an instant.

Jack had turned against the law and become an outlaw, riding with whatever gang he'd found that would take him. He obviously carried a lot of guilt about things he'd done while with that gang. Evie vowed never to ask him about that.

Somehow, the men who would become Saints had managed to wake him up from his anger and turned him around. He'd become a vigilante, to stop men like the ones who had killed his family, backed by his band of brothers, until they'd been broken apart. Now he worked on the outskirts of the law, hunting bounties, still trying to keep innocent people from becoming victims.

Evie's heart swelled, with admiration and pain for his strength and for what he had been made to endure. Ethel was right. This was a good man, whatever he might say on the matter.

She rested her head against his back, and didn't care in the least what the gesture might imply. He probably didn't need the comfort after all this time, but she was determined to offer it.

It wasn't until they stopped for lunch hours later that either of them spoke again, but the silence was comfortable. Jack was opening a can of food with his over-sized knife when she broke the silence.

"Do you ever think you might have that again? A family, I mean."

"No," he said immediately.

"Why not?"

"I think a man is lucky beyond belief to have that even once. Twice in one lifetime? Believe me, God doesn't like me that much, and he's got good reason not to." Jack handed her the can he'd just opened and a spoon.

"But what if you did? Meet someone you fell in love with. Would you ride away from that because you didn't think you deserved it?"

"You ask a lot of questions. What about you?" he asked, opening a second can for himself.

"What do you mean?"

"You had a nice life; comfortable, wealthy, privileged. You ran off and wound up running a whorehouse. Odd way to go. Why?"

"Privilege means different things for different people. For my father, it meant he had anything he wanted because he had money and power. For me, it meant I was his property. Another asset for him to invest. He tried to marry me off to a fellow politician for some political favor or other almost before my mother was cold in her grave. I had fallen for the farrier's son, and he offered to take me away. We'd run off together, get married, and live a free life."

"A farrier's son? Really?" Jack asked, his gray eyes showing his amusement.

"Yes, really," she said with a glare. "He was everything I thought I wanted. He was handsome, charming, rebellious, everything a strong-minded girl could ask for."

"You didn't get married," Jack stated, rather than asked. She was impressed with his insight.

"No, I didn't. I caught him in bed with another woman. So I broke his leg with a chair, and the other woman's husband, who happened to be the town sheriff, ran him out of town."

Jack burst into laughter, causing her glare to darken.

"And why, Mr. Hannity, is that funny?"

"Think about that one from my seat, darlin'. Daddy was rich, wanted you to fit into his lifestyle the way he thought you ought to. You ran off with a poor boy who claimed he wanted to rescue you. The curr cheats the first chance he gets. None of that is funny, but in response, instead of breaking down and turning into a sobbing wreck like any reasonable woman would do, you break the poor bastard's leg with a chair and have the sheriff run him out of town." He laughed again, shaking his head. "You are one hell of a woman, Evelyn Delano."

"I'm not at all sure if I should thank you for that remark," she said, eyeing him.

"Oh, believe me, it's a compliment, darlin'!" he

said, still laughing.

"I'll take it as one, then," she replied.

"All right, so the brothel?" he encouraged once he'd calmed himself. She sighed.

"That one was easy. I managed to take the savings Frank and I had gathered before running away, and with the sheriff's help, got a loan to buy the old saloon. The place was pretty run down, so I got a good deal. It didn't take long to fix it up and get it opened, though. Once good booze was available in town again, it got popular mighty quick."

Jack watched her, face passive, but eyes still shining. She was glad he was getting so much amusement out of her own difficult story. It was nothing like his, she admitted, but it had sure seemed a terrible tale when she was living it.

"Anyway, a gal comes into town one day on the stage. She was a mail order bride, come to be wed to her new husband. Trouble was, the man had died two days before from pneumonia. They weren't wed, so she didn't get a penny of his money. So here she was, stuck five hundred miles from home, with no money, no place to stay, no friends, and no family. She didn't want to go home, she had nothing left there, either. So I give her a place to stay and have her help out around the bar. I find out some time later that she's been soliciting men for months."

Jack was grinning again.

"Had a bit of a row over it, but in the end she convinced me she was doing it entirely of her own free will. I was paying her decently, and giving her room and board, so she wasn't desperate for the money or anything like that. She offers me a cut, and trying to get out from under the loan fast as I could, I let her keep at it. Next thing I know, word has spread and I've got four girls living upstairs, and paying me rent from their work. Jump forward a few years, and I've got six girls and a bouncer, and the approval of the local sheriff, since all my girls are clean and doing the job because they want to, not because they have to. We all make a pretty decent living, and nobody gets hurt."

Evie didn't know why she felt the need to justify her slightly questionable moral actions to a man who had killed men with his bare hands and run for some time with a gang of thieves and killers. But she did. He chuckled again and shook his head.

"Tell that to Parsons," he said, laughing again.

Chapter Eight

For the first time in a long time, Jack wasn't sure about his path anymore. Things had been so simple before he'd met Evie. Ever since he'd heard the womenfolk back at the wagons call her by her nickname, he couldn't stop thinking of her as Evie. It suited her, in a way he couldn't quite explain.

He'd known she would be trouble the moment he saw her storm into her saloon, fire raging in her eyes. Jack had been totally wrong about what kind of trouble she was going to be.

Well, he corrected as the pain in his arm reminded him, she was a whole lot of that kind of trouble, too. That wasn't what worried him, though. What worried him was the fact that for the first time in his life, he felt like he was being unfaithful to Lucy.

Jack had been with a few other women over the years, but none of them had been anything more than a convenience arrangement for the both of them. But now, for the first time, his heart was divided. Evie drew him in like nobody had since

Lucy, and the feelings gave him no end of guilt.

Lucy wouldn't be angry with him, he knew that much already. At least, not for this. He'd done plenty she'd have been angry with him for, but not this. This would be what she wanted for him; that he find someone else, and settle down so he wouldn't be lonely.

Jack hadn't really ever felt much in the way of loneliness, but he wondered now if maybe that was because he'd closed himself off from so many of his deeper thoughts and emotions. It was too much, and a man could get killed riding the range if he let himself get too emotional.

Evie made him emotional. She made him angry, made him frustrated beyond reason. When he'd seen Hound riding after her, she'd made him afraid. And when she laughed and smiled at him, she made him happy.

He had truly surprised himself back there with that family. Jack hadn't opened up like that in longer than he could remember. Not since Lucy and the children, for absolute certain.

One of the little girls at the wagon train had reminded him of Jacqueline, his daughter. Her name brought back a flood of emotions. And William, his son. Still so small, but he'd just started laughing at things that startled him. It was the most amazing sound in the world, when your little one first learned to laugh.

Jack grit his teeth. He'd told the Saints about

his family once. Only once. It had been enough. They'd been supportive and sympathetic, like good brothers should be, but he hadn't been ready to really reconnect with that time in his life, so it had been told without much emotion.

When Evie had brought it out of him, Lord knew how, he'd felt the dam start to break. Everything he'd held back had started to come rushing forward. And for some reason, it had been easier to handle than he'd thought it would be.

Maybe it had been the time that had passed. He had still had to pause a few times and keep himself composed, but telling her, feeling it again, had opened something in him.

No, he knew. Evie had opened something in him even before that. He was laughing, joking, playing with the children… all things he hadn't done in years. Jack had joked plenty with the Saints, but it was different than it was with Evie.

He found himself thinking about her all the time, thinking about how unusual she was, how much he enjoyed her company when she wasn't making him completely coon-crazy. Jack had even had the thought enter his mind that maybe he didn't want to collect this bounty.

He looked up at the dappled light filtering through the trees above. The foliage was much thicker here, with a lot more trees. It wasn't quite a forest, but it wasn't too far from it.

Confounded woman, he thought without much

conviction. She'd put a bullet through his arm, but he was suddenly wishing she'd put it through his head. Things had been so easy. Find a good bounty, chase the criminal, catch them, get paid. Life was simple.

He spent most of his time alone, and even when returning with a bounty, there wasn't much in the way of chatter going on, aside from his bounties throwing enough cussing at him to make the flowers wilt.

Jack liked being alone. Nobody to pretend for, nobody to have to put up with. Except he liked putting up with Evie.

It would never work, he knew. A gal like Evie wanted to run her business and live her own independent life. That was why she'd really run off from her pa. And why she'd ended up running a brothel. She wanted her own life, her own way. No woman like that would want a man involved, getting things all muddied.

That was why she'd never married after she'd busted up Frank. He smiled at that. He could very easily see her taking a chair and beating the fool broken while he lie naked in his own bed with another woman. Maybe she'd realized then that she couldn't really have her own life with a man around. Too many complications.

Evie was like himself, he thought. She didn't like complications. Evie *was* a complication, he thought sourly.

"You ever get arrested?" she asked suddenly.

They'd been riding quietly for hours since lunch. Silence with her had become comfortable. Neither of them seemed to need to fill a void with idle chatter. They chattered plenty, but it was never because one or the other felt a driving need to break the silence. Jack smiled at her question.

"I've been in jail a time or two," he admitted.

"For robbing stages?" she asked. He could hear the teasing tone in her voice, and he chuckled. He felt her grip shift slightly around his middle and he noted the warmth in his chest growing again.

"No, ma'am. For public drunkenness."

"Must have been expensive. You seem like a man than can take a whole lot of liquor before getting yourself sloshed," she said. He could hear the smile in her voice.

"Sure, but I didn't mind. I had lots of money from robbing stages," he said with a teasing grin as he turned to look at her back over his shoulder. She laughed, and he couldn't help but laugh along with her.

"You don't seem like the type to drink much, though," she said in a considering tone.

"Not anymore. Jarrett got me out of that. I have a sip now and then, but nowhere near enough to get myself drunk again. I don't like losing control."

"I'd have guessed that about you," she agreed.

"How about you? You run a saloon. I'll bet

you've had your fair share of whiskey."

"Not my poison. I love applejack, though. I got into a bottle in the liquor cabinet when I was young. Drank half the bottle before passing out in the closet under the stairs. Took them hours to find me. I sure got a whipping then," she said with an amused chuckled.

"Little Evie all drunk on applejack. I can see it now," he laughed.

"Evelyn," she corrected, then clarified. "I was little Evelyn, since my father insisted that ladies did not have nicknames."

"Sounds like a stiff," he stated flatly. She laughed lightly.

"That's a mighty kind way to put it, yes."

"No wonder you don't much care for going back to him. Well, that and the forced marriage," he added as an aside. Glancing at her back over his shoulder, he couldn't help but ask, "Was he really going to force you into a political marriage?"

"Sure as the day is long," she agreed.

"And here I thought we weren't part of the British aristocracy anymore."

"Try telling that to my father," she said ruefully.

"I'd rather not. I've met the man, if you'll remember. I'm fair certain that man could railroad a herd of buffalo into doing what he wanted, if there was money in it."

"You've certainly got a good measure of the man. That's him all right."

"Why don't you just leave again?"

"Oh, I aim to," she said firmly. "Won't be easy the second time, though. He'll likely have more than a few private enforcers hired to keep an eye on me, and will have all of Topeka's law enforcement officers watching, just in case I try to make a break for it."

"But you're going to try anyway?"

"You can bet your last dollar on that," she agreed. Of course, she would, he thought as he rolled his eyes.

"You're crazy as a coon, you know that, right?"

"Coons got nothing on me, Mr. Hannity," she said with a laugh.

"Jack," he corrected.

"We're not that friendly," she retorted.

"You called me Jack once," he pointed out.

"I did nothing of the sort!"

"You most certainly did. Right after you shot me."

"Oh," she said softly, surprised. She apparently hadn't realized she'd done so.

"It ain't gonna hurt none if you call me Jack."

"No, thank you. We're not friends until you agree not to return me to my father."

"You want me to turn around and take you home? We're closer to your father now than to your saloon. Besides that, there's five hundred dollars waiting for me at your pa's."

"You're a terrible person," she said irritably. He

didn't blame her.

"Every man, woman, and child within five hundred miles in any direction who knows me can testify to that."

"The good folk back at the wagons don't," she smugly pointed out.

Jack opened his mouth, then closed it again. He considered that for a moment. She was right. He'd been a very different man back there than he had been in a long time.

"Just trying not to raise suspicion," he finally said.

"You're a liar, Mr. Hannity."

"And a thief, and a rogue, and a brute, and probably a boor, too."

"Let's not leave any of those out," she agreed.

"As long as we're on the subject," Jack began, ready to take a few shots at her, too, but someone else took a shot at them first.

The bullet hit a tree off to the side, sending a few small shards of bark whistling past.

"Oh, good," Jack said dryly as he urged Patriot into a gallop, "things were starting to get too peaceful-like."

He looked back over his shoulder and past Evie, trying to spot the man who was shooting at them. He didn't see a man, he saw seven. Most were riding hard, though they were still a fair distance off. Another bullet tore past from the man with the long rifle who was trying to fire at a gallop. No wonder he'd missed twice, Jack thought.

Turning back around, he caught movement to his left, and saw another three men angling in from the side. They were much closer.

Jack drew his Colt and aimed across his body. The three men wove through the trees, making a clear shot for more than a split second difficult. One of them raised his own gun, but Jack fired first. The man fell, and the other two veered off slightly.

Another bullet hit a nearby tree from behind.

"Jack," Evie said, her growing fear evident in both her voice and her use of his first name.

"Don't worry, darlin'," he said as casually as he could manage, "This ain't nothing more than a little scuffle. Just stay in tight to me and…"

A man came out of nowhere to one side, leaping through the air and slamming into Jack and Evie, taking them both down off Patriot's back. Patriot, without a rider, stopped running and came back toward Jack.

Jack was occupied, however. As they landed hard, Jack twisted sharply and pulled the man totally clear from Evie. The man swung at Jack, but he got an arm up to block and slammed his own fist into the man's jaw. Without much leverage, the blow only slightly dazed the man.

Jack's eyes scanned the approaching men. The odds weren't good.

"Evie, mount and ride hard south!" he yelled.

At a hard ride with a light rider like Evie, they

were only about ten minutes north of the nearest town. If she could make it there before they caught her, she could get help. Jack had meant to skirt wide of the town, but she needed the help more than they needed anonymity. The enemy had found them already anyway.

"What about you?" she cried in a panic.

"I'll be along, go!" he yelled as he blocked another punch, throwing another of his own. "Go!"

Evie mounted fast and turned Patriot southward, kicking her into a full gallop. The two men nearing from the side were coming in fast, and changed direction to follow Evie.

Shoving the man back a few more inches, he snapped an elbow up and into the man's temple. Knocking him cold, Jack shoved him off with a grunt of effort. Grabbing his pistol from where it had fallen, he aimed and fired, one of the two men falling like his strings had been cut.

The other man had reached Evie, and his hand snaked out to grab her. Jack held his breath as he focused, squeezing the trigger gently. The gun's sharp retort rang through the trees, and the man fell. Four down, seven to go, he told himself, rolling to his stomach and raising the gun toward the other approaching men.

Three bullets left in his Colt, and seven men coming fast. Jack just hoped he had bought Evie enough time.

Evie rode harder than she ever had in her life. She was a passable rider, but running full tilt through the trees was not high on her list of things to attempt. Of course, neither was being shot. She tried to spare a glance back for Jack, but Patriot jumped a fallen log and she found herself clinging for dear life instead.

One of the men had nearly caught her, but Jack had brought him down with a shot. He only had three rounds left in that gun, she knew. The others were close enough that he wasn't likely to have time to reload.

Had she just left him to die? She couldn't help but wonder, and for a long moment she considered turning back around. He'd be furious with her if she did, though. And she couldn't help but recall what had happened the last time she'd tried to help him in a pinch. Besides, she wouldn't be useful to him in the least.

She heard gunfire behind her, fading into the distance. Managing to look back for a moment, her heart sank as she realized that not only was Jack too far behind her to be seen through the trees, but that two of the men had apparently gone around to chase her, leaving the others to deal with Jack.

At least he only had five to deal with, now. Still only three bullets, though. She wondered briefly if

Jack could kill five men with three bullets. Leaning back down into the ride, she knew right now she had to worry about herself.

Evie heard one of the men behind her take a shot, and she flinched down low. She had no idea where the bullet went, but knew it hadn't hit her and that was all she cared about. Patriot hadn't changed pace either, so it wasn't likely she'd been hit.

Looking down, she saw the butt of the rifle in its saddle holster. This was a bad idea, she thought, even as she tried to wrestle the gun free. After another missed shot from the men behind her, she managed to get the gun into her hands.

For a long moment, she tried to figure out how to hold the thing and not fall off the horse. Finally, she held tightly to the pommel with one hand, holding the rifle with the other, awkwardly stretching it out behind her as she half-turned.

She pulled the trigger, no hope of aiming, and the kick of the rifle made her grip slip. Frantically, she let go of the pommel and lunged for the gun with her other hand. Just catching the barrel, she winced at its heat as she quickly tried to bring it back up.

Patriot jumped again, and the gun was jarred out of her hands as she snatched at the pommel again in a panic, ending up clinging to the horse like some kind of monkey. Great, she thought in irritation. One more thing for Jack to be angry with me about. Now I lost his rifle.

Cursing under her breath, she adjusted her position to a more secure one again, and risked a glance back. The two men were closer. Much closer.

She didn't know what Jack's plan was, but he'd told her to ride south, so she was riding south. She hoped he caught up soon.

With nothing to do but ride, she stayed low and tried to keep as many trees between her and her pursuers as possible. They fired a few more times, but she suspected it was more to keep her scared than any intention to actually harm her. There wasn't much chance of them hitting her at this speed in these trees, while she was working hard to keep a few between them all the time.

Evie rode for several minutes before suddenly reaching the end of the trees. Ahead of her stretched a long, sloping hill. At its base was a town. This must have been what Jack had wanted her to find. She broke out of the trees, realizing that in a few seconds, the men behind her would have a clear shot at her back.

The town was still a ways off, but she could see people. And so, Evie did what any self-respecting, unarmed woman in the prairie would do when pursued by hostiles. She screamed at the top of her lungs.

The piercing scream carried well down the hill, and several people looked up. It was about that moment that the men behind her broke out of the trees, and one took a shot at her. Thankfully he missed again, but it made the situation immediately clear to the folk below.

At the sight of a screaming woman racing toward the town with two men riding hard behind her, obviously trying to shoot her, several of the men ran inside nearby buildings and came out with guns.

The first few shots were enough to send the men spinning back around and racing for the treeline. One of the townsfolk fired again and one of the two men fell. The other made it back into the trees as Evie made it into town. She didn't slow for several seconds until she could manage to look back and reassure herself that she was not still being chased.

"Ma'am?" a gravelly voice called. She stopped Patriot and took a moment to try and catch her breath. It was coming in short, sharp gasps.

"Thank… you!" she said to the men coming toward her, between gasps.

"What in the devil is going on?" the older gentleman with the gravelly voice asked. He had a badge on his shirt. The sheriff, she realized. He and the other man held guns. The third, some distance behind, was clearly a preacher, his black shirt and white collar a near-universal symbol of his position.

"Those men… trying to kill… me," she tried to get out, still fighting for breath. She took the sheriff's offered hand and dismounted.

"Whatever for?" the sheriff asked curiously. It

was obvious that not much interesting happened in this town, she thought. The sheriff seemed more confused than concerned.

"They want to get… at me to get to my… father."

"Who's your father, then?" he asked.

"Lieutenant Governor Warren Delano," she said. The sheriff blinked in surprise.

"The Lieutenant Governor? Well then, I'd say that makes a right fair amount of sense," he said.

She smiled her thanks as the preacher came up to them. Something about his eyes caught her attention. They looked like Jack's, she realized after a moment. Not the same color or shape, but they had the same hawk-like intensity, the same dark depths. He smiled back, and the smile was warm and friendly.

"Were you riding all alone out here, ma'am?" asked the sheriff. Evie started to feel her breath steadying.

"No, sir. My friend is still back there. We got knocked off the horse. He still had five men coming at him when he made me mount up and ride. Only those two came after me. The others will come soon though, if Jack doesn't manage to kill them."

"Think he might have?" the sheriff asked in surprise. Evie thought about it, then nodded.

"I think he might. I hope he did, anyway. I need some men to ride back with me to get him."

"What kind of man can handle five armed men

by himself?" the sheriff asked.

"Jack Hannity could," the preacher said, to her astonishment. His powerful gaze regarded her, as he waited for her to confirm his guess.

She stared at him and he smiled slightly without humor, as her reaction fully confirmed his suspicions. Behind the smile, though, she could see the same flickers of regret that Jack got sometimes. The preacher looked slightly paler than he had a moment ago.

"You know him?" she asked in wonder. The preacher nodded.

"I know the man well. We were friends, some years back." Something clicked in Evie's mind and she smiled brightly.

"You're Jarrett!" she said. Now it was his turn to look surprised.

"Reverend Thomas Jarrett, yes, ma'am. He spoke of me?"

"He did," she agreed. "Will you come with me to get him?" He shook his head slightly, causing her smile to falter.

"No, the sheriff and a few of the other men will ride out. You need gunmen, just in case Jack didn't manage the others."

"Aren't you…" she started, remembering what Jack had said about Jarrett, but the man was already shaking his head.

"I don't use guns," he told her with a warning glance. She took the hint and shut up.

"All right. Sheriff, we need to go now. He might need our help!"

Jarrett shook his head again.

"By now, Jack is either dead, or already dealt with those men and is on his way here. Us hurrying won't help much," he paused, listening. "Besides, from the sounds of the others back at the town line, somebody is already riding out of the trees. Shall we go see if our friend Jack has beaten the odds once again?" he smiled softly at her, and she nodded. She liked this man already.

The pair headed for the edge of the small town, the confused old sheriff and his deputy following behind like a puppy dog.

She saw the half a dozen men from the town with rifles leveled at a man riding slowly down the slope, arms held high. She recognized him instantly and couldn't keep the relieved, excited smile from spreading across her face.

Jack stopped about fifty feet from the line of men and slowly dismounted. Evie ran toward him, pushing through the men. Even she couldn't miss the broad smile that he flashed when he set eyes on her.

"Jack!" she cried as she ran to him. Reaching him, she threw her arms around his neck and hugged him tightly.

For a moment, Jack didn't move. After a long moment, he put his arms around her as well. As if the small act had given both permission, they relaxed into one another completely. Jack's cheek rested atop her head, arms around her as if they belonged there and always had.

Evie's heart fluttered as she realized they fit together perfectly, like their bodies had been forged as a matched pair. The thought caused her cheeks to color. Letting him go, she took a step back, a little awkwardly.

"I'm glad you made it," she said awkwardly, embarrassed at both her actions and her thoughts about them.

"I was thinking the same about you, darlin'. I got scared when I saw that other man come riding back."

"I got scared when I left you with five men and three bullets!" she laughed. He grinned.

"I had nine loaded. Still had Hound's gun."

Evie had forgotten about that one. She smiled brightly, for the first time glad that he'd robbed the man.

"Oh," she said suddenly as she remembered something she desperately wanted to tell him, "you'll never guess who I found!"

"Who?" Jack asked, confused, looking up at the line of men, now watching the pair's awkward display.

Evie could tell the instant Jack spotted Reverend Jarrett. It was fascinating watching his expression rapidly shift as his emotions played across his face. It was incredibly subtle, and she doubted most would have noticed it.

First came the look of astonishment, then a moment of confusion, then excitement, finally settling on a slight tightening of his jaw that showed his uncertainty. Well, she thought as she looked back at Reverened Jarrett, this should be interesting.

Once Jack took a step forward, something it obviously took an act of will for him to do, he approached the other man quickly and Evie hurried to keep up. She didn't want to miss a second of this. Now face to face, the men locked eyes. There was a tension between them like a pair of tomcats, each unsure if the other intended to attack.

Without warning, Jack moved. Reverend Jarrett didn't flinch, and Evie suspected he was half expecting Jack to hit him, and was willing to take the hit. What the hell had happened, she wondered again. Jack didn't swing, though. His arms went around his old friend, gripping him tightly.

Reverend Jarrett barely hesitated, returning the embrace with the slightly bigger man. From where she stood, she could see the relief on Reverend Jarrett's face. A weight had been lifted from his shoulders, and even Evie, who had never met the man, could clearly see it.

After a moment, they pulled back and Jack clapped the reverend on the shoulder, grinning broadly.

"Now here's a face I never expected to see here in the middle of nowhere. I'd heard you were preaching in some one-horse town someplace up in the Dakotas."

"I've gone where the Lord needed me," the reverend said with a smile. Jack's eyebrows dipped subtly.

"Take it easy with that stuff, Thomas. Let's keep it civil, all right?"

"Don't worry, Jack. I'm not gonna preach at you."

"Good."

Reverend Jarrett looked pointedly at Evie, one eyebrow raised. Jack got the hint and introduced her to his friend.

"Thomas, this is Evelyn Delano," Jack said. Jarrett tipped his flat, wide-brimmed hat at her.

"Pleasure, ma'am."

"Likewise," she replied with a smile.

"Now," Jack interrupted, "if you don't mind, I need a drink and to sit down. It's been a long day."

"Come," Reverend Jarrett said, "I'll take you to the sheriff's office, where you can make a statement about what happened today, then we can go to my church. I'll make you two something to eat and we can catch up a bit before you turn in. The hotel has plenty of rooms available, so should be no trouble getting a couple of beds."

"Thanks, Thomas," Jack said, his tone implying more than just thanks for the food and lodging recommendations. Reverend Jarrett looked at his friend for a long moment, then nodded once.

As the reverend turned to lead them to the church, Jack looked down at Evie. She thought his look was intended to be a warning about her behavior, but there was no sincerity to it. Which made sense, she knew, since every time she hadn't listened to him, bad things had happened.

She had no intention of causing a fuss here, especially not with his reunion with one of his fellow Saints. This promised to be very enlightening indeed.

Chapter Nine

Jack followed Jarrett back to the church, still trying to get a handle on the fact that he was walking alongside Thomas Jarrett, once gunslinger, now preacher. He'd known Thomas had been pursuing religion after the Saints of Laredo had ridden their separate ways, and had even run into him a few months later, when he'd been preparing to enter the seminary.

That conversation hadn't ended well, with Thomas basically insisting that either Jack join him in the seminary to atone for his life of sin, or he'd burn in Hell for all eternity. It had ended in a yelling match that had nearly come to blows, and Jack had stormed off.

He'd heard Thomas had become a priest and been preaching someplace, but he'd honestly never expected to see him again. As long as Thomas kept the preaching out of things, this could be a good chance to reconnect.

Jack and Evie had given their statements to the sheriff, shown the man their paperwork and Jack's badge, and then gone back outside to meet up with Thomas again where they followed him to his small church at the very far edge of town.

As they entered the church and headed toward the back, Thomas stopped to genuflect in front of the cross and altar. Jack grit his teeth. It wasn't that he had anything against God. Quite the contrary. He just objected to the way the church told him he should act and feel about God. Jack had always thought such things were intensely personal, and never had taken kindly to anyone telling him how it should be done.

They moved through a door in the back of the chapel and entered the good reverend's private quarters. There was a small kitchen, with a small bedroom and a door leading out back. It was… cozy, Jack thought.

"Please, sit," Thomas said, gesturing to the small table and the two chairs. Sitting, Jack watched as Thomas brought another chair in from the bedroom. He didn't sit, though. Instead, he poured them each a drink, then started a fire in the small iron stove and began to cook.

"How long have you been here?" Jack asked, wanting to talk, no matter what it was about. He took a sip. The whiskey wasn't overly strong, but it wasn't mostly water, either.

"Two years, next harvest. I had just finished seminary when the old pastor in this town passed away. They were pretty desperate, or they wouldn't have brought in a green preacher like myself. This town needed a lot more than Reverend Leonard, anyway. He spent more time drinking than preaching."

"You content?" Jack asked directly.

Jack was never much for skirting around the issue at hand. Evie looked at him in surprise, looking a little embarrassed by his rudeness. He wasn't worried. Thomas knew him better than any man alive, excepting only Storm-Chaser. They'd long passed the point of Jack's directness being considered rude.

Thomas nodded without hesitation.

"Unquestionably, yes. In a lot of ways, I wished I'd done this fifteen years ago. I learned a lot during that time, though. I wouldn't have been ready, then. All part of His plan."

"I couldn't do it," Jack said, shaking his head.

"Oh, you'd make a terrible priest," Thomas said. Jack laughed.

"Not what I meant."

"I know," Thomas replied with a grin.

"The whole settling down thing," Jack clarified. "I don't know if I could make it through a day without getting shot at or someone trying to bash my head open."

"He has that effect on people," Evie interrupted. Jack gave her a sharp look, but was privately amused. She certainly enjoyed taking jabs at him. Thomas laughed.

"You don't have to tell me, Miss Delano," Thomas told her. "I've wanted to do both to him more than once over the years."

"Me too, and I've only known him a few days," she replied.

"Thank you," Jack said wryly. Evie laughed and he felt his chest tighten.

"I actually did shoot him, though," she said casually. Thomas snapped his gaze over to her in surprise, his grin broadening. Jack rolled his eyes and took another sip of the whiskey.

"I'm glad you're not a better shot, then," he said. "I still need time to try and save his soul."

"Actually," Evie clarified, "if I were a better shot, I wouldn't have hit him at all. I was aiming for the other fella. Besides, it was just a flesh wound." Thomas laughed again.

"Keep this one, Jack. I like her."

Jack looked down at his glass. If only it were that simple. He felt another surge of guilt as he thought of Evie, then of Lucy. And then of his contract to deliver her to her father.

"She's my bounty," he said simply. Again, Thomas looked over in surprise.

"Your… I beg your pardon, ma'am, but you don't strike me as the lawless sort."

"I'm not," she said, giving Jack a glare.

"Her father wants her home for her protection. Seems he's upset a few folk that might want to hurt his little darlin' here."

"Really? Who's her father, if you don't mind my asking?" Thomas asked.

"Warren Delano," Jack replied.

"The lieutenant governor?" he asked, looking their way, eyebrows raised. Jack couldn't help but smile. At this rate, his old friend's face might get stuck looking forever surprised.

"That's the one."

"I heard about the ruckus over the coal mine. That what this is about?"

"Sure is."

"That what today was about?" Thomas asked, gesturing toward the part of town where they'd shot one of the men.

"Sure is."

"I'll be," Thomas said, half to himself. He brought some fried potatos and sausage over to the pair, and they dug in hungrily.

"It's a bit peculiar," Thomas said casually, pausing to take a bite from his own plate as he sat. "You two seem awfully cozy for a bounty hunter and his charge. You cuddle up with all your bounties, Jack? Or just the pretty ones?"

Jack was a little embarrassed. That hug had been all Evie, until it suddenly wasn't. He'd been shocked when she'd hugged him, and completely unsure what to do. Almost purely on instinct, he'd put his arms around her, and it had been like the sun had suddenly risen in his world again. In an instant, everything was illuminated. The embrace had turned warm and comfortable, his cheek resting atop her head at the perfect height.

It couldn't happen again, he told himself sharply. But it had happened, Thomas had seen it, and he'd have to deal with that.

"Just the pretty ones," Jack replied, taking a sip of his whiskey. Evie looked at him critically.

"And are there a lot of pretty ones, then?" she asked him, tone carrying a warning.

"I don't know, 'Pretty Boy' Anderson was mighty pretty. Hence the name," Jack mused, liking that he was getting her riled for a change.

"And did you hug him?" she asked coolly.

"Well, it was more of a bear-hug as I wrestled him down off the bar, but it was mighty cozy."

"There's something wrong with you," Evie said. Jack and Thomas both laughed.

"Damn right," Jack said, the same time Thomas said "Lord knows." They grinned at each other.

"So," Thomas said after a pause, "you taking her back to Topeka?"

"That's right."

"Then what?"

"And then I was thinking about going after Martin Reese and his cousin."

"Didn't he kill a bunch of folk during a train heist?" Thomas asked.

"That's the one."

"Good bounty?"

"Seven hundred dollars," Jack admitted.

"How much for the pretty one, here?"

"Five," Jack said. Evie gave him another dirty look.

"Five hundred for her? And seven for Reese?"

"And his cousin," Jack clarified.

"Seems a bit off," Thomas said, musingly.

"All depends on who wants them. Her pa is a politician, willing to pay more than a few dollars to protect his little girl. The people killed on that train were all Pinkerton men, so Pinkerton is the only one who really cares much. And seems they don't care enough for a hefty bounty for the fellas who killed their men. Cheaper to just hire new men."

"Lot of work for seven hundred, taking in two men," Thomas pointed out, raising a brow.

"Not so bad," Jack replied with a shrug. "I brought in the entire Wilson gang, few years back. That was a lot of work. Worth two thousand dollars, but per head it was only about two hundred."

"How on earth did you wrangle that many heads at once?"

"Kept them all tied and stacked in the back of their own wagon. Eighty miles with them bouncing and jostling all over one another in the back of a wagon that needed some major repairs. A few bruises, a few splinters, nothing serious. They were begging to be taken off my hands by the time we rode into Wichita, though," Jack told him, laughing. "Jail would be more comfortable."

"You could come back here," Thomas said.

Jack paused.

"What do you mean?" he asked, though he knew full well what his old friend was implying.

"After you deliver the lovely lady to her father," Thomas told him, "you could come back here for a spell. Might be nice to enjoy a bit of peace. I can make arrangements for you. Mr. Dawson has a spare room since his son got that job in Topeka. He'd even let you give him a hand on the ranch if you felt like making yourself useful. No need, though. It'd just be… nice to have you around again for a while. Give us time to catch up, since I'm sure you can't dally around here too long this run through. Not with you being chased and all."

"Thanks, Thomas, but I don't think I'd relax much, laying idle like that."

"I told you that you could help with…"

"That's not what I mean, Thomas. You want to save my soul, so do I. Only I don't think spending my time in a lonely church chewing the fat with your silent and invisible God is the way to do it. I catch the bad guys, Thomas. That's what I do. I save lives by scraping the scum out of the pond. I need to make amends for what I've done, not just pray for forgiveness."

He hadn't meant to get so intense, but between Evie and the unexpected reunion with Thomas his emotions were running a lot higher than usual. Thomas was quiet for a long moment, and Evie stayed blessedly silent. She was watching intently, though. Enough to make a man uneasy, he thought to himself. Looking for an escape opportunity, or a weak spot? Not going to find one this way, darlin'.

"Last week, I helped with a barn raising," Thomas said, almost as if thinking out loud. "The new barn is gonna to let the Ferguson family near-double their production from their farm. Lord knows, they need it with the new baby coming. Week before, I helped Mr. Howard with some planting, since he'd fallen ill. Delicate seeds, only a very small window to plant if you want a good fall crop. He'd have missed it, I reckon. Two days gone, I spent some time at the widow Riley's place, helping her with a new calf. Poor gal's never dealt with the young'uns before, had no idea what to do. Soon, her son won't have to bring milk from his farm to provide for her. His own family can scarce spare it, so that'll ease a burden for them both."

"I'm not sure what you're getting at, preacher," Jack said, putting a bit of bite into the term. Thomas was unmoved by it, he just leaned forward and made his point sharp and clear.

"Catching criminals is great, Jack. That does a world of good for a lot of folk. But we spent so much time, you and me and the Saints, trying to make the world a better place with big, grand deeds, but there were always more cattle rustlers, bandits, and killers to be chased. What if we were treating a symptom, Jack, not the disease? What if the best way to really make the world better is with the little things. A helping hand to a neighbor, a kind word to someone in pain, a listening ear to a friend, raising a child or two to be good, kind people. What if that's how we really make the world better? Not just today, but in the future."

Jack was quiet, letting the words sink in. Thomas continued.

"There's lots of ways to help folk, Jack. Catching criminals ain't the only way to redeem yourself."

"I ain't looking for redemption, Thomas," Jack said, but he wasn't at all sure that was true. "I just can't sit around knowing men like that are still riding. It ain't right."

"Neither is running away from your own happiness because you don't think you deserve it," Thomas said softly. Jack looked down into his glass. "Just think about it, Jack. Just a week or two, after you've escorted Miss Delano home. Longer if you take a fancy to a bit of breathing room, but at least that long. You've got my word, Jack, I won't say a word to you about God if you do."

"I'd pay good money to see you go a couple of weeks without mentioning God."

"I didn't say I wouldn't mention him, Jack, just not to you." Thomas flashed the grin he'd been known for with the ladies, one he'd heard an elderly socialite they'd rescued once refer to as "quite cheeky".

"I'll think about it, Thomas."

"That's all I'm asking, old friend."

"Thanks for the chow, but we should get to the hotel and get ourselves a couple of rooms," Jack said, downing the last of his whiskey.

Thomas nodded and stood along with him. Evie followed suit, but looked sad to be going. I'll bet, he thought. Nothing like watching your captor's soul being laid bare by a bloody preacher.

"Miss Delano, maybe you can move on ahead and get yourself those rooms. I'd like to speak to Jack for a moment or two alone. It's straight ahead from the church, then left at the blacksmith. Can't miss it."

"Of course," she replied.

"Now, wait," Jack protested.

"Don't worry, Mr. Hannity," she said with a soft smile. "I've no mind to try running off tonight. Not after seeing what kind of folk really are trying to get at me. Trust me, I'm not going anywhere."

Evie gently touched his arm with the tips of her fingers. The touch sent a tingle running the length of his arm. Not willing to give in completely, he frowned at her.

"Preacher, you got a Bible we can make her swear on?" he quipped. Thomas grinned.

"Sure do, but I don't reckon that's necessary. I believe her."

"Thank you, Reverend," she said with a warm smile. Jack sighed.

"Well, all right. But you run off again and I'm

going to shoot you in the leg so you can't run anymore, you hear me?"

"Yes, pa," she said with a playful smile. He shook his head as she left the room.

"I like that one," Thomas said, sitting back down.

Jack sat down as well, cautiously. He had no idea what Thomas wanted to bring up in private. Lord knew he'd brought up enough in front of Evie.

"She's a spitfire. I don't think I've ever had a bounty give me so much trouble," Jack replied.

"Love will do that," Thomas replied.

"What in the Sam Hill are you jawing about?" Jack snapped. Thomas shrugged.

"I know you, Jack. And I've performed enough weddings to know what love looks like. You look at her that way, under all the glares and scowls. She looks at you that way, too, you know."

"That's ridiculous," Jack denied. He'd thought he had seen it a time or two himself, though, and couldn't deny it quite as firmly as he wanted to.

"It's not, and you know it. I saw the way she hugged you when she found you hadn't been filled full of holes. And I saw the way you hugged her back. That was your first, wasn't it?" Jack didn't deny it, and Thomas continued. "I'm not saying you should rush off and marry the woman right this moment, I'm just saying you need to consider the possibility that just maybe settling down wouldn't be a terrible thing. You'd make a fine husband and a wonderful father."

"Tried that once," Jack reminded him.

"I know. And it was taken from you. It was a tragedy, that's undeniable, and I don't mean to imply it was anything but. I just want you to ask yourself; would Lucy want you spending your life running away from happiness on some desperate quest to avenge her? You already did that, Jack."

"That's not why I do this, Thomas," Jack said, his tone taking on a warning edge. Thomas ignored it.

"Like hell, it's not," he swore. The words coming from the mouth of a man in a priest's raiment seemed a little jarring, though Jack had heard far worse from Thomas Jarrett in years past. Jack stared at his friend. "Every time we roped another one, I saw the look in your eyes. Every time another killer was taken off the street, I saw how much better you slept. It's vengeance that drives you, Jack, not salvation. Justify it all you like, but that's plain truth."

"And if it is? Nobody cares why I hunt these people, just that they're locked away. And I guarantee my motivations don't make one lick of difference to the lives I save doing it." Jack replied, pushing down a surge of anger at his friend for prying in where he hadn't been invited.

"I'm sure they don't," Thomas agreed, "but it makes a whole world of difference to you. Stop chasing her ghost, Jack. Lucy wouldn't want you to do this to yourself day after day, year after year. All she ever wanted was for you to be happy, and you've been running from happiness since the day she died, because you're afraid it'll get taken away from you again. Being happy isn't a sin, Jack. It isn't a crime against your departed wife. I don't want to see you throw away your chance any more than she would have. I don't know Miss Delano from Eve, but I know the look in her eyes. She loves you, Jack. And you love her, sure as the sun sets. Don't be so all-fired stubborn. Take her home, see her safe, then spend some time with her. Before or after you come back here, don't much matter, but at least explore the idea that maybe you and she might have a real chance at something most folks spend their whole lives searching for."

Jack stared at his empty glass for a time, trying in vain to deny every word out of his old friend's mouth. Finally, he pushed back his chair and stood.

"That's a whole bushel of talk about love and happiness from a man who can't marry. Good night, Thomas. Thanks for the whiskey."

With that, he turned and left the church.

He strode briskly to Patriot, unhitched her, and mounted up. He rode her at a trot out of the churchyard, then slowed to a walk. He needed a moment to clear his thoughts before dealing with Evie again.

Every time he tried to deny his friend and brother's words, thoughts of Evie entered his mind.

Every time she touched him, his skin tingled. When she looked him in the eyes, his spirit warmed. When she laughed, his world moved. She broke down walls within him so old he'd forgotten that they even existed.

Lucy, he thought in a silent prayer to the woman he'd loved, still loved, what do I do?

He hitched Patriot to the post and grabbed the bags, heading into the hotel. Evie was waiting for him in the lobby. She looked a little concerned, as if she too had been wondering with some trepidation what Thomas had wanted to speak to him about.

The place was nice, though small and simple. She was sitting in one of the three chairs near a corner of the small lobby. Nobody else was in the room.

"Well, you didn't run," he said to her. She smiled.

"I told you I wouldn't, Mr. Hannity," she answered.

"Jack," he corrected.

"We're not that friendly," she replied. He neglected to point out that she'd done so twice now, and the sky hadn't fallen in on her.

"Got the rooms?" he asked. She hesitated and he frowned. "What happened?"

"Well, I only got one room…" she said uncomfortably.

"What? They all full up?" he asked in surprise. This couldn't be happening, he thought. This was the last thing he needed right now.

"No," she said slowly. She wasn't telling him everything. He could hear it in her hesitation.

"What… happened…" he said slowly and clearly.

"They had plenty of rooms, and we can still get another one if you say we have to, but…"

"But what?" he asked, irritated. She looked up at him, and her eyes were moist with unshed tears.

"I've never been shot at before," she said. He noticed her hands were shaking. "I don't want to be alone."

Her explanation was spoken in a bare whisper, and she was clearly trying to fight back tears. The look on her face and tone in her voice broke all his restraints. Dropping the saddlebags, he reached out and took her in his arms, holding her closely.

Evie cried and shook, the emotions and fear of the day finally overwhelming her. He'd been shot at so often it barely troubled him anymore, but Evie was from a cultured childhood, and had, until recently, lived a relatively peaceful life.

She'd shot at others before, as in the case of Parsons at her saloon, and at him once while aiming for Hound, but that was a very different thing than being shot at. He remembered turning into a useless, shaking child after his first shootout. It had taken several drinks to settle his nerves.

That had been a long time ago, though. It hadn't even occurred to him that it might rattle her so much. He couldn't blame her; not at all.

He gently stroked her hair and held her close as she sobbed. For several minutes, they were the only two people in the world. She, lost in the overflow of her fear and stress; him, lost in an inner struggle about the women he now cradled in his arms.

After a time, she calmed herself and pulled away, wiping at her eyes and pointedly not meeting his. She turned away from him. His heart lurched. He couldn't deny it anymore. Thomas was right. Jack loved her.

"I'll get another room," she said, her embarrassment and anger at herself evident in her voice.

Jack reached out and caught her hand. As she looked up at him in surprise, eyes still wet, he stepped forward, putting them close again.

"One room will be fine, darlin'."

Chapter Ten

Dear Lord, what am I doing? Evie's thoughts were in a total panic. It had seemed perfectly reasonable when she'd requested the single room, but now that she had talked to Jack about it, all she could think about was how terrible an idea it had been.

She'd let her fear overcome her reason, and then had completely broken down in front of him. He'd been blessedly tolerant of the outburst, and had even been kind enough to comfort her. His steely gray eyes had been soft and understanding as she'd turned at his touch on her hand.

Evie forcibly reminded herself that this was the man who had abducted her, and was still stubbornly taking her to her father, whom she despised, and who would likely marry her off within a week of her being back in Topeka.

It didn't matter, she knew. All that mattered was that she loved him. Circumstances wouldn't ever allow them to be together, but she'd stay as close to him as she could be until he took her home.

They'd likely make it there by nightfall the next day. She wondered if he'd unload her at the first opportunity, or wait until the next morning.

Evie had no idea, but intended to be as close as she could be to him for as long as possible. Maybe when she escaped from her father again, assuming she could manage it before getting stuck at the altar with a man she hadn't chosen, she'd try to find him.

That was ridiculous, she told herself. She'd just go back to her saloon. Jack didn't want her. Her heart had crashed into her gut when he'd told Reverend Jarrett that he would never settle down. She'd been right all along; Jack wasn't the settling type. He needed danger, needed his open range.

Anything else was a fantasy, and she knew it.

Jack opened the door of their room, and stepped back, gesturing her grandly in with a slightly playful smile and a mocking bow. She couldn't help but grin back at him as she threw him a curtsey and entered the room.

He followed her in, closing the door behind. The room was nothing special, and looked remarkably like the rooms above her saloon. One bed, one small table, a small washstand, and a single chair. There was a small chest at the foot of the bed for clothing.

Jack didn't bother with it, though. Evie watched, fascinated despite herself as he set the saddlebags on the table and moved to the washstand, pouring a bit of water from the dented metal pitcher into the plain ceramic bowl.

He scrubbed his hands for a moment, then dumped the water out the window between the washstand and the small table and chair before pouring a bit more water into the bowl. He scrubbed his face for a moment, drying both hands and face on the small towel.

She'd noticed before that Jack was surprisingly clean. He obviously took it seriously, and likely washed as often as he could, she realized. He might even have called for a bath if he hadn't been on a job.

That thought conjured the inevitable image of him undressing, causing color to flush up into her cheeks and heat to spread through her body in a pleasantly uncomfortable manner. She looked away for a moment just as Jack turned toward her.

"All yours, if you want it," he told her as he moved to the table and removed his long coat, draping it over the back of the chair, hanging his hat on the wall hook beside the table. He ran his hands through his hair and stretched.

She couldn't take her eyes off him. He looked at her questioningly, and she realized he'd noticed her staring. Of course he did, she cursed at herself. *You were staring like a complete loon.* Taking the excuse, she moved to the washstand and began cleaning herself up a bit as well.

By the time she'd finished, he'd taken off his boots and gun belt, and suddenly looked for all the world like a comfortable, settled-down kind of man.

Images of the man now before her sitting in front of a fireplace, playing his harmonica for a couple of children on the rug at his feet flashed into her mind, and the warmth flooding her body became a different sort. This man here was a man she could see as a father, and as a husband. A man who smiled and laughed, a worked on a farm or a ranch raising a family.

She'd seen glimpses of this man back at the wagons when he played with the children, but she truly thought it was something about his removing the gunbelt that seemed to change everything about him. His entire demeanor was different.

A knock came at the door, and the gun came into his hand from the belt on the table so quickly that she wasn't entirely certain it hadn't jumped there all on its own. There he was, she thought sadly. There was the outlaw-turned-bounty hunter. Jack was once again the iron-cold, gritty, dangerous man she'd first been abducted by.

"Yes?" Jack called cautiously.

"Mr. and Mrs. Hannity?" a youthful voice from outside tentatively replied.

Jack gave Evie a dark look, and she flushed from embarrassment. It had made sense when she'd requested the single room that they appear as a married couple. She regretted that decision more than anything else she'd ever done in her life up to this precise moment, however.

"Yes?" Jack finally answered.

"My pa asked me to bring up some food for you."

Jack tucked the gun in the back of his pants and moved to the door, opening it. There was a young woman on the other side, holding a tray of food and two mugs of what was likely a weak ale. Jack gave the girl a smile, and Evie watched with both amusement and sympathy as the girl visibly flushed at the handsome face turned so warmly her way.

"Well, thank you, darlin'," he told her, bringing a girlish giggle from the proprietor's daughter. "Tell your pa we're much obliged." He reached into his pocket and handed the girl a couple of coins.

"Oh, sir, this is too much," she replied, surprised.

"One for the food, and one for you," Jack answered with a wink. The girl's blush looked like it was about to set her face afire. Evie almost laughed. She shook her head at him as he closed the door.

"You shouldn't do that," she said with a chuckle.

"What?" he asked, looking confused as he moved to set the tray of food on the table beside the saddlebags.

"Flirt with the poor young thing like that," she replied.

"What do you mean?" Jack asked, picking up a roll and biting into it.

"Now don't give me any of that nonsense,"

Evie retorted, moving to grab the other roll herself. "You can't possibly be so dense that you don't know what you do to women."

Jack's eyes took on a mischievous sparkle and the edges of his lips twitched upward. Evie knew immediately she'd said the wrong thing and was about to dig herself into a deep hole.

"And what exactly do I do to women?" he asked.

"You know perfectly well, Mr. Hannity."

"Jack."

"We're not that friendly. I just mean to say that a poor young girl like that has no defenses against a charming, handsome smile." She could have kicked herself. Evie couldn't believe she'd now essentially told him she found him charming and handsome, and that he had a strong effect on her.

"Charming and handsome, hmm?" he asked, stroking his stubbly chin thoughtfully. "Yes, I can see how that might have an effect. I don't quite see how that's a problem, though."

"Come now," she replied, trying now to regain some stable footing in this rapidly-deteriorating conversation, "you flirted quite on purpose, as I'm sure you do with all the young girls you come across. I'll wager you leave a trail of crushed women in your wake." Somehow, none of this was coming out how she intended, and she felt sure she was deeper into that hole by the word. Jack's teasing grin told her she was quite right.

"I wouldn't go that far," he answered. "I only flirt with the pretty ones, after all."

"Don't go pretending you never flirted with me," she accused. Again, he took it quite differently than she'd intended. His grin broadened and one eyebrow raised slightly as he waited for her to read into her own remark. She felt her blush rising again and scowled at him.

"You're turning things all around, Mr. Hannity. You might be passingly handsome and charming enough when you choose, but let's not forget you're also a boor, a rogue, and a kidnapper of defenseless women." Jack laughed at that.

"Darlin', you're anything but defenseless. You've been a harder collar than any bounty I've ever chased."

Evie blinked at that, surprised.

"Have I, really?"

"I've caught more than forty hard criminals, not counting the small fish, and not a one has managed to shoot me, let alone steal my horse or turn an entire saloon full of men against me in the blink of an eye." He took his last bite of the roll and moved to take a piece of the roast beef.

Evie stared for a moment, then laughed herself.

"Well, let this be a lesson to you, Mr. Hannity. Us women-folk aren't as helpless as you men-folk seem to think we are." She took a bite of her own roll and gave him a self-satisfied look.

"Didn't I just say you were anything but

helpless?" he laughed. "Lord knows, you women are dangerous as vipers. I don't think I'll ever take a contract again if the subject is a woman."

She chewed for a minute as she thought about that last comment.

"Have you caught women before?" she asked. The thought hadn't actually occurred to her. His grin turned teasing again and she scowled. "That's not what I meant. See? You're an absolute boor. I meant have you ever been contracted for a bounty on a woman before?" Jack laughed lightly and nodded.

"Yes, ma'am. I sure have. Plenty of women breaking laws, too. They're always trouble, though never as bad as you've been. I still have another full day's ride to bring you in, and I have every intention of asking for a bonus from your father for this fiasco."

"Are you seriously still going to hand me over to that man?"

"I made a contract, darlin'. A man doesn't have much out here except his word."

"Even if I made you give me your word you wouldn't?"

"Couldn't happen. I gave my word I'd bring you to your father, and I will. What happens after that is fair game, but no amount of money or persuasion will keep me from delivering you to your father."

Evie had to admire his integrity, but his firm

assertion that despite their growing closer he had every intention of going through with this quickly killed her mood for banter with him. She finished eating in silence, and he was wise enough not to interrupt it.

Evie yawned widely almost as soon as she finished the last swallow from the mug. She hadn't realized how tired she was. Standing, she looked at the bed, then at Jack. He read her thoughts easily enough.

"Don't worry, you can have the bed. I've got my bedroll here, I'll just set myself up over there."

"Are you sure? I am your bounty after all. Wouldn't you prefer tying me to the table or something and taking the bed yourself?" her tone was intended to be cutting, but even to herself she just sounded petty. He smiled without humor.

"I'm sure," was all he said.

"You turn yourself right around while I get in bed, then," she snapped, angry more at herself than at him. He stood and turned his back on her. Rather than standing and waiting, however, he began moving furniture. "What are you doing?" she asked.

"Barricading the window. Can't have you slipping out in the middle of the night."

"And what about the door?" she asked, curious despite herself as she watched him stack the wash stand atop the table and move them both in front of the window. After a moment, she remembered she was supposed to be preparing for bed.

"Don't you worry about that," he said, "I'll run my bedroll right in front of it."

"You think of everything, don't you."

"Obviously not," he muttered.

Rather than try to figure out what he meant, she began removing her shirt and britches, leaving herself in only her under clothes. She hurried into the bed, pulling the blankets high around her neck. The bed was passable, but to her, at that moment, it felt incredibly luxurious.

"All right, I'm covered."

Jack turned around and gave her a look she couldn't read. Picking up his bedroll, he began setting up his own sleeping arrangements, directly in front of the door, as promised. Without warning, he began unbuttoning his shirt.

"You could warn a lady, first," she snapped, looking away. He turned to face her directly, and she couldn't resist a glance back. His shirt was half-undone, the strong lines of his chest visible.

"Oh, pardon me, ma'am. I forget sometimes what effect I have on women." His tone was flat, but his eyes had started to sparkle again. She almost grinned despite herself.

"I'm only concerned with propriety," she replied again.

"Of course," he said, and began undoing the next button.

Despite her complaints about propriety, she didn't look away. His eyes were down, watching his hands, but hers were firmly on him. He slid the shirt off his shoulders and down his arms before giving the shirt a shake and hanging it over the back of the chair with his coat.

Evie watched, unable to look away.

With a sidelong glance at her, eyes full of mischief, he reached for the button on his pants.

"Don't you dare!" she shrieked, and he burst out laughing.

"You're right, that's some effect!" he said through his laughter.

She scowled at him and purposely rolled over to face the wall. He laughed another few moments, then she heard him chuckling as he blew out the lamp and slid into his bedroll.

This was going to be a long night, she silently told the darkness around her. Jack sighed contentedly and she felt a tingle run up her spine.

A long night, indeed.

Chapter Eleven

Jack lay awake for a long time. She was angry with him, he knew. She had a right to be, he was taking her someplace she didn't want to go, to the care of a man she didn't want to see, to be sold into a marriage she didn't want.

That last bothered him more than anything else. Turning in a criminal or two didn't phase him in the least, but turning over an innocent woman for what amounted to just short of full slavery didn't sit well with him at all.

More than that, the thought of her marrying at all set a pit in his stomach, all the more so since it wouldn't be a happy marriage.

You don't know that, he told himself. Arranged marriages have been around far longer than voluntary ones, and a lot of them grow into love stronger than many voluntary marriages ever did. Love could be learned.

Jack didn't need to learn it, though. He already loved her. And someone else would be her husband. Against her will.

He sighed again and rolled over as if to rid himself of the discomfort of the thought. It didn't help.

You could turn around and ride the other way, he thought, except you'd be breaking your word. He didn't have a lot of convictions left in his life, but needing to help keep bad things from happening to good people, and keeping his word were two of the strongest.

That was a huge part of the problem, he realized. Those two convictions were at war with one another. He was delivering an innocent into the hands of someone who planned to sell her off, because he'd given his word to do so.

Jack hadn't known, of course, that that's what her father had planned for her. He didn't actually know now that's what her father planned, just that it's what he'd planned that caused Evie to run away in the first place. Besides, she was just going to run away again.

He couldn't go back on the contract. It would not only go against his principles, it would destroy his reputation as a bounty hunter. He had more than enough money to retire comfortably, but he literally had nothing else.

Rolling over again, he lay looking toward the middle of the room when something moved past the window, shadow sliding across the thin curtain. He was out of bed with his gun in hand in a flash. Something clanked faintly outside, and he moved carefully toward the window.

There was a little light leaking around the single old curtain, and it was steadily moving, as though a shadow was moving slowly across the window.

Jack crouched low, inching forward, gun ready. Down to one side of the window, he leaned up just enough to tip the corner of the curtain back with the barrel of his pistol so he could peer outside.

A stablehand below, in front of the stable, was walking around a pair of horses, holding a lantern in one hand. The faint sound of other voices below the window told him that the hotel had just picked up a pair of late night travelers.

The movement on the window was a result of the lantern light being broken and shifted around as the stablehand had been walking behind the animals. Jack took a breath to calm the energy that had flooded his system when he'd caught the movement out of the corner of his eye.

He eased the hammer back down on his gun so as not to wake Evie and stood, turning back to return to bed.

Evie was sitting bolt upright in the bed. She must have sat up the same time he'd rolled to his feet, or he'd have heard her sitting. She stared at him in panic, tears on her cheeks.

Jack tucked the gun into the back of his jeans and moved toward her. She stood from the bed and took the last two steps toward him in almost a run. Jack put his arms around her as she began to cry silently into his chest.

He stroked her hair and spoke gently.

"Easy there, it's just the stablehand putting away a couple mares. Nothing to be afraid of," he whispered. She clung tightly to him, and he felt a surge of protectiveness. He held her even closer and closed his eyes. "It's all right, darlin'," he murmured, "I'm here. I'm right here."

She cried for another minute before she slowed, taking deep, slightly shaky breaths. He kept whispering assurances and stroking her hair until she finally eased back. He let her go, feeling like part of him was pulling away with her. She pulled back just enough to look up at him, eyes and face still red and wet.

"I'm sorry," she said in a slightly broken voice.

"Don't be," was all he said, one thumb wiping away the tears still on her cheeks. He suddenly became very aware that her hands were on his chest, and he still had one hand around her back, the other gently touching her face.

For a moment that stretched on forever, they simply locked eyes with one another, the warmth of their bodies seeming to build. Rational thought gone, Jack let himself really feel it.

Impulsively, he leaned down and his lips touched hers. For the briefest of moments, she tensed in surprise, then seemed to melt into him. The saltiness of her tears was fresh on her lips, the heat of her body warm and comforting against his.

For one brief instant, his thoughts kicked back in and he began to pull back, but she pressed closer to him and the troublesome thoughts disappeared.

The gentle kiss deepened, his lips parting slightly as hers did. He could feel her breath mingle with his, and the lightest touch of her tongue on his lips sent a thrill up his spine. Despite the gentleness and slow nature of the kiss, there was an intensity to it that set Jack's whole body tingling. Years of pent up emotion poured into him, and nothing could have pulled him from her at that moment.

Her hands slid along his chest, then down around his sides and onto his back. Pulling gently, she guided him toward the bed as his hands felt the gentle curves of her skin beneath the light shift she was wearing.

Realizing where she was going, Jack stopped and pulled back.

"Evie, I can't…" he murmured.

It was too much for him, he knew. He'd been with other women since Lucy, but somehow this was different. This was something more, and crossing that line felt wrong, like he was betraying Lucy. Evie just shook her head.

"I just want you to hold me," she whispered. "Just lay here with me. Please?"

His resistance gave way, and he let her pull him into the bed. She slipped under the blanket, taking his hand to pull him in beside her. Jack's eyes ran along her body as she moved down to the bed, the short, light shift sliding effortlessly along her skin as she moved, showing every curve in silhouette.

Moving down to the bed himself, he slid under the blanket and moved up against her, his other hand placing the gun gently on the floor. As she pressed against him, he put his arms around her. Her head nestled against his shoulder, warm cheek against his skin, her hand gently running along the powerful lines of his chest.

Jack could feel every inch of her against his skin, fitting up against him like she was made for it. Rather than simply arousing, though he couldn't deny that it was, it felt comforting in a way he didn't fully understand. In her arms, he felt a warm, open, and total comfort he'd not felt in more years than he cared to count.

Gently as a whisper, he kissed her forehead and lay back, closing his eyes.

He knew this couldn't last. For a thousand reasons, it couldn't last. But he'd have this, now, tonight. Just himself and Evie, giving each other the comfort they both needed.

Just for tonight.

Evie woke slowly, peacefully, and feeling more comfortable than she thought she had in her entire life. It took her several minutes to consciously wake up enough to realize why. She felt the warmth of a strong body beside her, big arms wrapped protectively around her. His scent filled her nose as she breathed deeply, stretching a little. Her hand moved along his stomach, where it had apparently been for some time.

Jack was still soundly asleep, she knew as she listened to his breathing and felt his chest rise and fall steadily under her cheek. The muscles of his stomach, even when he was relaxed in sleep, were flat and just tight enough to hint at the strength in them.

Her hand explored the curves around his sides and up to his chest, feeling his skin and hair, feeling the gentle arc of muscles now used to cradle her gently in his powerful arms. She could lie here forever, she thought.

He'd have to remember to change his bandage when he woke, she thought as she looked at the torn strip of his old shirt wrapped around the upper part of his arm.

So focused was she on the feeling of his skin and muscles that it took her some time to realize his breathing had changed. Pulling back, she looked up at him, to find his gray eyes looking down at her almost tenderly.

"That's a hell of a way to wake up," his deep voice rumbled softly. Evie felt that thrill run through her abdomen at the depth and richness, and now the softness, of his voice.

"Sure beats waking up to prowling Indian

scouts," she replied with a smile. His grin was slow and peaceful, like she felt at the moment.

"It does at that," he agreed.

Neither made a move to get up, so Evie lay her head back down on his chest for several minutes, just enjoying the contact with him.

"You're a lot nicer to cuddle with than Pretty Boy Anderson," he said suddenly. Pulling back sharply, she looked up at him. The playful, teasing light in his eyes told her all she needed to know, and she burst into laughter, giving him a playful shove.

"Dear Lord, I should certainly hope so," she replied. "Come on, I'm hungry."

He chuckled, but let her climb over him to get out of the bed and get her clothes. She stood dressing, and was nearly done before she remembered he was watching. Turning, she gave him an embarrassed look.

"You shouldn't do that, you know," he said as she locked eyes with him.

"What?" she asked, trying to pass the whole thing off as casually as possible.

"Dress in front of a poor old man like that. You can't possibly be so dense you don't realize the effect you have on men," he told her. His eyes practically sparkled with his amusement. She blushed furiously.

"What effect might that be?" she asked, as she began buttoning the riding shirt.

"Try changing your clothes in front of me

again, and you'll find out," he said. His tone was joking, but there was a throatiness to it that caught her attention.

Despite his reluctance to get too close the night before, she could see the spark in his eye, behind the sparkling amusement and mischief, that spoke of distinctly more heated thoughts than another night of cuddling.

Her blush grew hot, and she felt that heat flood her entire body. She turned away before she said or did something she'd regret. Maybe another day, she thought, but not just now. They'd only just entered this territory, after all.

Evie could hear Jack get out of bed and move to get his shirt. She turned and made a point of watching him, quite certain this was a terrible idea. Turnabout was fair play, and all that, she told herself by way of justification.

He picked up the shirt, and noticed her eyes on him. Turning so she could watch the entire show, he shook out the shirt again and slung it over his head and around his shoulders, his arms sliding into the sleeves as he did so. He didn't even wince as he stretched his wounded arm out like that.

The heat built in her as she watched the ripple and flex of his muscles with the smooth, graceful movement. He began doing up the first button, and laughed as she turned away.

"I need breakfast," she said, pulling on her boot and kicking his bedroll aside to get out the door.

What did this mean, she thought as she headed down the narrow hallway. The warmth and intimacy he'd shown last night, and that kiss… she shivered from the thought. How she'd love to explore his talents in that regard in more depth.

Perhaps, she thought, they could. His flirting a few moments before had showed an openness and level of relaxation she hadn't see in him before. Who knew what would come next for them?

Could there be a them? Suddenly, she wasn't so sure it was impossible. There was no way he could dump her off with her father after last night.

"Good morning, ma'am," the man behind the front desk said as she passed by. It wasn't the proprietor, but this gentleman seemed friendly, so she smiled back at him.

"Good morning. Does your kitchen serve breakfast?"

"Certainly," he replied, gesturing toward the door to the common room. "Right through there, Josephine can get you all fixed up."

"Thank you," she answered, heading through the door.

She took an empty seat, which wasn't hard since the room was almost entirely empty. Only one other couple was in the room, talking quietly and happily in the far corner. Only a moment later, the young lady from the night before came in from the back door.

"Morning, ma'am," the girl said. Evie got a

better look at her this time, and estimated her to be perhaps nineteen. A little older than she'd first guessed, but not by much.

"Good morning. Are you Josephine?"

"Yes, ma'am. Can I get you some breakfast?"

"Please," Evie replied enthusiastically.

The food the night before had been excellent, and the thought of breakfast that good set her stomach rumbling. She felt more relaxed than she had in days, and that seemed to simply make her hungrier.

"Will your husband be joining you?" the girl asked innocently, but Evie caught the eagerness in her eyes. She couldn't help but smile, all the while suppressing the thrill in her heart at hearing him referred to as her husband. Jack had smiled once at the girl, and she was already smitten. Evie knew how she felt.

"I believe he'll be along shortly," Evie replied. "Can you bring a plate for him as well?"

"Sure can," the girl said with a nod.

Josephine glanced at the door, as if hoping Jack would walk through that very moment. She looked distinctly disappointed when he didn't. She gave a little curtsey to Evie and headed back toward the kitchens.

The girl was sweet, Evie had to admit, but Jack was spoken for. It was another minute or so before Jack arrived, and she spent the entire time toying with the idea of asking Jack to come back to Falls

City with her, maybe stay with her for a while, just to see where things might go.

She saw him and her heart fluttered. He was fully dressed again, and carrying the bags, but despite the coat, hat, and gun, something about him still seemed different. The man she saw wasn't the hardened gun-slinger, nor was he entirely the warm, happy man she'd seen that morning. The man who approached her now was someplace in between. It suited him, in a way she couldn't describe.

He sat across the small table from her and smiled.

"You order already?" he asked. She nodded.

"Your little lady will be along in a few minutes," she teased. Jack grinned.

"Do I need to be on my best behavior?" he asked. "You know, so we don't have any swooning girls dropping our breakfast?"

"You flirt all you like," she replied, feigning coolness. "It's not like you're spoken for." Her words were in direct contrast with her own thoughts of a few moments before, but Jack didn't know that.

"True," Jack said, musingly. "Maybe I'll see if she's of marrying age. She's a pretty little thing."

Evie scoffed.

"Simply disgusting. You're nearly old enough to be her father," she pointed out.

"Exactly how old do you think I am?" he asked, his expression surprised.

"Old enough to know better," she retorted. He

grinned.

"All right, so maybe it has been more than a summer or two since I was young enough for a roll in the hay with a filly like that." Evie made a face at him.

"You're disgusting," she said again.

"And charming," he reminded her.

"Mildly. Sometimes," she corrected. "This is not one of those times."

Jack just chuckled as Josephine came out with a tray of food, just as she had the night before. Evie smelled the sausages even before she saw them, and her stomach let out an audible rumble. Jack laughed and looked at her incredulously.

"Easy there, darlin'. Wouldn't want anyone thinking you were anything less than a perfect lady."

Evie rolled her eyes.

"I'll have you know, I've won the belching contest three years running at my saloon," she told him.

"Ah yes, there's my delicate flower," he quipped. Her heart leaped at his words, the possessive 'my' practically singing to her.

"Good morning, sir," Josephine said shyly.

"Mornin'," Jack replied with an incredibly charming smile, tipping his hat to the girl, who blushed. "My goodness, darlin', that smells divine."

"Thank you," she said, her color deepening as she set the food on their table. Evie stifled a laugh.

"Here," Jack said, handing her two coins

identical to the ones he'd given her last night. The girl looked up at him in surprise, and he winked. She smiled brightly and curtseyed before heading back out of the room.

"Absolutely dispicable," Evie said with a laugh as she snatched one of the sausages.

"Just brightening a sweet girl's day," he pointed out with a wink at her this time, moving a fork to the eggs on his plate.

More than one, Evie thought, the warmth having settled with apparent permanence in her chest as she looked across at Jack. Nothing could spoil this mood.

Chapter Twelve

Jack was lost. He'd always been lost in one way or another, ever since his family had been taken from him, but now he knew it.

His internal war was raging wildly, his duty battling fiercely against his heart, his doubt warring with his hope. He didn't deserve her, he knew. Men like Jack Hannity didn't deserve to be happy. The best he could hope for in life was to help protect others so they, in turn, might find some glimpse of the happiness he'd once taken for granted.

He knew she deserved better. She deserved a man who would put her first above all else. Jack couldn't do that. What he'd said to her was completely true, and all a man out on the trail really had was his word.

But what if you weren't on the trail, that infuriatingly seductive voice in his head asked. He could settle down, get married, try again. It didn't matter. The one thing he'd never lost in all his years running from the pain of loss was his word. Without it, he was nothing. He meant nothing.

Evie deserved better, he thought for the hundredth time that morning.

He tried not to sigh as he watched the low trees pass slowly by. The sunlight was warm, without being hot, and a faint breeze blew across the plains, rustling the fields and the leaves of the low trees. Another idyllic day, he thought with a trace of annoyance.

They had ridden out right after breakfast, several hours later than he'd intended to leave. They'd both slept in, and it was no wonder. He hadn't slept that well in a very long time indeed. If she'd slept half as well as he did, it certainly explained her bright and happy mood.

Jack and Evie had bantered and joked all through breakfast, and the entire experience had seemed so *normal.* It was as if that was what life was supposed to be like, he thought. Just a couple having a nice breakfast, enjoying one another's company. She did enjoy his company. He wasn't so dense as to have missed that.

It couldn't be love, though. She'd remember how angry she was with him soon enough, once it really registered to her that they were once again drawing closer to her father. They had left late enough that they might not actually make it into Topeka until the next morning.

Maybe that was her plan, he thought idly. Perhaps she was just playing with him, trying to delay their trip until she could find a good chance to escape. Except she'd already missed one good chance earlier that morning when they'd stopped for a break.

Jack had gone into the trees for a few moments, completely forgetting that he'd left his prisoner unbound, with his horse. She'd already stolen his horse once. And his rifle along with it, that she'd dropped while riding away from the men who'd attacked the day before.

He was still irritated about that, but it would be easier to get a new rifle than to try and find out where she'd dropped it on her mad dash through the trees. Not that he hadn't considered more than once going back to find it after delivering Evie to her father. Jack liked that gun.

Jack had come back a few minutes later to find her still sitting beside the bush, leaning back on her hands and watching the clouds. He'd had to pause for a moment, just to watch her. She'd seen him watching after a moment and smiled at him.

We could just ride off, he thought to himself. Right now, ride off into the distance and leave everything behind. He knew the problem with that, though. If he did, not only would her father's enemies still be looking for her, but the other bounty hunters would be looking as well.

She was still in danger. And while she was safer with him than she was nearly anyplace else, she'd be safest under the eye of her father's hired security force, and the local law enforcement her father no doubt had on the payroll.

He sighed and approached her. Opening his mouth to speak, something caught his ear and he froze.

"What?" she asked curiously, seeing his expression.

"Shh," he told her.

She did so, and he listened. After a moment, he moved around the large bush they'd been taking shade under and looked across the plain beyond the bush. It was mostly empty, a huge, swaying expanse of long grass rolling with the wind, dotted with an occasional shrub poking out.

After a long minute, he heard nothing. Shaking his head, they had mounted and continued on their ride. Something had seemed off, but he couldn't see or hear anything to indicate what.

Now, again, he was contemplating just riding off with her. He could take her so far away that there was no way anyone would find them. He had connections both far out west, and south of the border into Mexico. They could vanish without a trace.

Getting there would be the hard part, though. Who knew how many miles they'd have to ride before they were outside the search radius of people her father had sent to find her. His word aside, staying with him was more dangerous for her than returning her to her father. And he couldn't risk her like that. Not for him.

He fought back another sigh, not wanting to alert her to his inner struggle. She rode comfortably behind him, arms loosely about his waist as she enjoyed the passing scenery. As if reading his mind, however, she spoke words that set his heart lurching.

"Come back with me," she said suddenly.

"Pardon?" he asked, though he'd heard her clearly.

"Come back with me, to Falls City. You can use one of the rooms over the saloon if you want. As long as you like."

Jack was quiet a long moment. He could feel her growing more tense by the moment.

"I can't," he answered simply.

"Sure you can. Just turn Patriot around, and we'll go back the way we came. I'll even give you free whiskey, as long as you don't go too polecat wild with it."

"I can't," he repeated, more urgently.

"Forget my father," she insisted. "He won't keep his word to you, why should you to him? You know what'll happen to me if you take me to him. I'll be married inside a week to some old politician to further my father's goals. What about my goals? What about what I want for my life?"

"I have a contract, Evie."

"Oh, right, your precious contract," she said bitterly. "I had thought after last night... I just thought..."

She trailed off, totally unaware of the struggle in his mind at that moment.

"Thought what?" he asked finally, both desperate and terrified to hear what she would say.

"Nothing," she said, voice subdued.

"It can't work, Evie," he said after another long pause. "Ladies like you and trail-riders like me? Two different worlds."

"I run a brothel," she said wryly. "I'm not exactly high and mighty."

"That's not what I meant," he protested, but wasn't sure he could explain any better. "You just.. you deserve better."

"I want you," she said, her voice soft, but sincere.

Jack had never dreamed he'd ever hear a woman say that to him. Not again. Not in the way that she meant it. He wanted her, too. Madly, intensely, desperately.

His heart screamed at him to sweep her into his arms and kiss her, then enthusiastically turn Patriot around and ride hard for Falls City, but more than anything, his fear for her safety quieted that part of himself.

"They'll kill you, Evie," he replied simply. He couldn't trust himself to say anything else. "Your father has a small army of private security, and I'm sure the Sheriff, on his payroll. They can protect you better than I can."

"I'd be a prisoner! So, forget the saloon," she

cried. "We could go anywhere, I don't care! I don't want you to leave." He could hear the desperation in her voice.

Jack couldn't be sure it was sincere, though. He had a pit in his stomach as he thought about the possibility that she was saying what she thought he wanted to try and get him to not take her to her father. He couldn't blame her, considering what he was likely bringing her back to, but it didn't make the cut any less deep to think he was being played.

Even if she wasn't playing him, it didn't matter. He needed to bring her back to her father for her own safety. The men who wanted to hurt her father had already shown they had no qualms about putting a bullet through her. Jack felt sick at the thought.

"I can't, Evie."

"You and your damned word!" she cursed. "Fine. You know it's wrong. You know what will happen to me. If you can live with that on your shoulders for a few hundred bucks, you just keep riding south."

Jack closed his eyes and said nothing, keeping Patriot steadily moving south. It wasn't about his word anymore. He'd feel less guilty about breaking a contract than he would about effectively selling her into marital slavery.

It wasn't about his word, or the money anymore. It was about keeping her safe. Jack had seen what was after her. He suspected there were several more bands the size of the one that had attacked them, roving the countryside and looking for sign of her.

"I gave my word," he said, latching on to that one point as his lifeline, his one tether to hold him to the course he knew he had to take. He couldn't protect her from roving bands of killers forever out here. It was the only justification he could give her without admitting how he felt. It wasn't enough and he knew it. Her next words, spoken softly, but with venom, pierced him more than any bullet ever could.

"Damn you, Jack."

Chapter Thirteen

Jack was damned, and he'd known that all along. From the moment he'd seen his wife lying in a pool of her own blood in the middle of the dirt road leading away from their house, he'd known he was damned. The house had been too burned to even find what was left of his children to say goodbye and give them a proper burial. He wasn't just damned. He'd already been living in Hell since that day.

Only the Saints had kept him from selling his soul entirely to the devil. Only his brothers had helped him find what was left of his sanity, and what was left of his virtue.

And then came Evie. A fiery, sharp-tongued angel who had brought a light into the darkest parts of his soul, illuminating things he'd thought gone forever. Then she'd offered him a life with her. Or the start of one, at any rate. A chance at a real life, at the very least. It was more than he'd ever dreamed he could have.

And Jack was turning it down. It was one of the

hardest things he'd ever done, refusing that offer. He'd given his word, and it was for her own good. She would never let herself be forced into marriage. Even if her father were trying to use her that way, a gal like Evie would never allow it to happen. No amount of threatening or coaxing would bring an "I do" from her lips against her will.

He wasn't bringing her back to be sold into marriage, whatever she said. She'd fight tooth and nail, like she always did.

It would all work out all right for her. And Jack would ride on, leaving her to find a better man. A safer man. Someone who deserved her. Not him.

In a thousand years, he'd never be worthy of her. He was a killer and a thief, or had been in not so long ago. A boor and a ruffian, as she kept accusing him, was the least of what he deserved to be called.

Her grip on him had become as loose as possible while allowing her to still keep her balance, and he'd felt her seething every step since they'd stopped talking. They needed to stop for some food, he knew, but he wasn't looking forward to it. The sun was high in the sky and had started to come down again.

Jack steered Patriot toward a small, rocky hill, and frowned when he saw it had no bushes or trees on the far side for shade. Nothing but more grass. Sighing, he stopped Patriot there and reached back to help Evie down. She pointedly ignored his offered hand and climbed down herself. He sighed again and dismounted.

Setting up a small lunch, she didn't speak a word to him. He took Hound's gun from the back of his belt, setting it to one side as he lay along the slope of a large rock and ate a leftover biscuit. Patriot grazed contentedly in the long grass nearby, and Evie sat with her back to him. Every bone in her body, every tiny movement screamed her anger at him.

It was probably better this way, he thought. If she was angry enough, she'd hate him. If she hated him, it'd be easier on her when he left.

Something suddenly felt wrong to him. The second time in a handful of hours. He opened his eyes with a frown, and listened. He couldn't hear anything. Turning his head, he pressed an ear to the stone below him. There was a dull rumbling resonating through the stone. Jumping to his feet, he climbed quickly up the low hill, and looked out over the plain.

In the distance, he could see a group of men riding hard their way. Cursing under his breath, he scrambled back down the rocky slope, and looked up at Evie, ready to call out to her.

Jack froze at what he saw. Evie sat in Patriot's saddle, holding Hound's gun, aimed directly at him.

"Evie, what are you doing?" he asked in astonishment.

"Leaving," she said coldly.

"This isn't a good…"

"I don't care," she interrupted, not letting him speak.

"You don't understand, there's a…"

"I don't care!" she shouted at him. His brows came down angrily.

"Evie, that's enough. We have…"

"We have nothing," she interrupted again.

"You think I couldn't draw and fire before you could shoot me?" he asked, glancing at the gun significantly.

"You wouldn't shoot me," she said, with such certainty that he wondered how exactly she knew that.

"You wouldn't shoot me either," he said confidently as he took a step forward. She cocked the hammer with an ominous click.

"I already did, once," she pointed out. "Nothing to stop me doing it again." Jack suddenly wasn't entirely sure she wouldn't shoot him a second time.

"Evie, we don't have time for…" he said as he stepped toward her again, beginning to gesture back toward the hill. Her finger slipped inside the guard and he stopped once more.

"Nobody is going to force me into anything, least of all marriage. I won't let you do it," she said. He heard her voice crack and his heart cracked along with it.

"Evie," he tried again.

"Goodbye, Mr. Hannity," she said firmly. "If I ever see you again, I'll shoot you." Turning Patriot sharply and kicking her into a full gallop, she rode away from him. Away from the riders too, to his relief, but it wouldn't buy her much time.

Jack cursed angrily, turning to scramble back up the hill. He stayed low so the riders wouldn't see him. They'd been some distance off, and you could see for miles on a plain this broad, but they were closing.

He dropped down again and thought. She was going to ride Patriot as long and hard as she could, to put as much distance as possible between them. He'd never catch her on foot.

Jack knew he was also at least five miles from the nearest town, the wrong direction. He needed a horse, but would never get to one in time to catch up with her any time soon. Oh, he'd find her eventually, that much was a given, but almost certainly not before the riders approaching did. Which gave him an idea.

He moved along the rocks toward one side of the hill. The riders were probably following their trail, so would ride straight toward the hill. If one of them got close enough...

Crouching into position behind one of the larger rocks, he waited. Another two minutes passed before the first of the riders passed him. He had estimated eight men in this group when he'd last looked. The first to pass was too far out. He heard more men passing on the other side of the hill, and hoped a few more would take this side. The second thundered past, also too far out.

Listening more than watching, he timed his move. At the last possible second, he leapt out from the rock, hitting the third rider to pass squarely in the side. The man went over hard, and Jack clung desperately to the saddle as he lay almost across it, taking a moment to regain his balance before lifting himself upright and getting his feet in the stirrups.

He heard a call of alarm from behind as the one man left behind him on this side spotted him. Luckily, the other men were spaced out enough that nobody seemed to hear the cry.

Jack slowed the horse, and the man thundered up beside him, reaching for his gun. Jack already had his out, but instead of shooting the other man, which would attract a lot of attention since nobody else was shooting, he swung back and slammed the man in the face with the butt of his pistol.

The man fell backward off his horse, landing hard. Jack cut toward the other horse sharply enough that the now-riderless horse slowed to keep from running into him. Jack kicked his own horse back into a hard gallop, leaving the other animal behind him, and moving toward the back of the group ahead.

He rode hard with the men for several minutes before he had another chance. Luckily, none of the others looked back at him. He rode up close alongside another of the men, and grabbed the man's face, slinging him backward out of his saddle. The man didn't even have time to cry out.

Five left, he thought to himself. He didn't know how many he was going to be able to take down before the others started noticing, but he was off to a good start. At least he had enough bullets now if they started shooting. He looked ahead and took stock of where they were.

There was an open stream not too far ahead, he knew. No tree cover, and the stream was narrow enough Patriot could jump it, but was too rocky to wade through. He seriously doubted Evie would jump it, though. She wasn't sure enough of her riding skills. Which meant she'd turn, he guessed. Whether she would have gone east or west, he had no idea.

Swerving sharply as he came up on another of the men, Jack leaned his shoulder in and slammed into the other man. With a heave of his shoulder, the men went sidelong out of the saddle.

The man's hand snapped out and grabbed the sleeve of Jack's coat. He held on for just a moment, but as he started to take a breath to call out for help, Jack yanked his arm free, and the man fell to the ground.

The other four didn't seem to notice. It wouldn't be long, he knew. Sooner or later, they'd hear the difference in the number of hoofbeats, if nothing else.

West, he decided. She'd have turned towards the sun. It was a guess, and he knew it, but it was better than nothing. These men would likely jump the stream, assuming Jack and Evie had done the same. They obviously didn't know Jack wasn't still with her.

Not long now, he told himself. He slowed the horse just enough to drift behind. When they were far enough ahead and approaching the stream, he banked west and leaned low to urge the horse to greater speed.

If he could catch her before they realized she hadn't gone that way, and if they could then cover enough distance before being caught, they might make it someplace safe before they had to stop for the night.

He had to catch her himself, first. If she kept riding the stream this direction, she'd eventually come to the railroad. He wasn't sure what she'd do at that point.

Almost idly, Jack wondered if she knew her hard riding away from him was actually taking her closer to her father, rather than away. With that thought, he reigned in hard. The horse stopped sharply, hooves digging up furrows in the soft earth.

Of course she'd know that, he realized, cursing himself for a fool. She wouldn't have kept riding this direction. She'd have tried to loop north again once she was out of sight.

Stupid, he chastized himself. Turning north, he

kicked into a gallop again. On the plus side, it meant their pursuers had probably been riding the opposite direction from Evie for some time now. Just as he had been, he grumbled to himself.

Jack took quick stock of the horse he rode. It was a good mount, and would likely ride hard for some time. He doubted this mare could keep up with Patriot over the long haul, but Evie was an inexperienced rider. Jack could catch her.

This horse also had a rifle in a saddle holster. Jack smiled to himself. Well, that was something.

He rode for what felt forever, slowing the horse whenever he had to let her rest a bit, but he never stopped. As he rode, he searched for signs of her, and cursed his own idiocy.

If she was hurt, he'd never forgive himself. Again.

Chapter Fourteen

Evie didn't know how long she'd been riding. She was in a narrow line of trees along this stretch of the stream, but that was all she knew. Her tears had blurred her vision for several minutes after she'd ridden away from Jack, and she'd relied entirely on Patriot to keep them from getting into any trouble.

Once she'd regained control enough to clear her eyes, she'd realized they were riding south. Grumbling to herself in frustration, she had turned Patriot west just before reaching a stream. Evie was afraid she'd get lost if she tried to navigate on her own, but remembered there was a railway running north to south, and it was west of where they'd been riding.

She honestly had no idea how far west, but was fairly certain it was there. If she found that, she could follow it north to the nearest large town, and could sell the gun to pay for a train ticket for her to get back home.

Evie had no idea what she'd do when she got

there, though. She couldn't stay, for several reasons. Everything had changed. She no longer wanted anything but Jack, but that wasn't possible. All she had left was her saloon, and the thought of going back and spending the rest of her days the way she had been existing wasn't appealing in the least.

Then there were the men after her. She couldn't endanger her girls or Ben by sticking around someplace she'd be easy to find. Not to mention her own danger, she thought wryly. She couldn't endanger herself that way, either.

For a time, she toyed with the idea of selling the saloon and buying a ranch someplace further west, but every time she pictured the ranch, Jack appeared there as well.

Her tears threatened to dominate her vision again, and she blinked several times angrily to clear it. Wiping at her eyes with one hand, Patriot hit a jarring step in his run, and it jostled her a little. The gun fell from the back of her belt to the ground below before she could react.

"That figures," she grumbled, slowing Patriot and turning her around to go back and retrieve the gun. She might need that. Besides, she was embarrassed that in her two escape attempts, she'd managed to drop her gun both times. She wasn't cut out for this kind of life.

Dismounting as she spotted the gun, she moved toward it. The movement came so fast, she didn't even have time to scream. The two men came out of nowhere, one of them grabbing her tightly as the other snatched up the gun in his free hand, the other holding a shotgun aimed at her.

"Afternoon, darlin'," the gap-toothed fellow with the guns said.

The term gave her a pang of longing for Jack that cut through her panic. The term reminded her now of him, though when this man said it, it felt greasy. When Jack said it, she felt warm and playful. She hated when people called her that anyway, but somehow it was different when Jack did it.

"Let me go!" she yelled, pulling pointlessly against the powerful grip holding her. She heard a deep, raspy chuckle behind her.

"We sure will, but not afore we get to yer pa's house. He's got five hunnerd dollars says we bring you nice and quick to him."

Great, she thought. From one bounty hunter to another, and it hadn't even been two hours yet. She really wasn't cut out for this kind of life.

"He won't pay," she said, trying to sound confident. It was possible that her father would try to weasel out of paying the bounty, whether she was returned or not, but Evie wasn't completely certain.

"A' course he will! He's the one offerin' the five hunnerd dollars!" Dear Lord, she thought. This one's a genius.

"I meant," she said slowly, as if speaking to a simpleton, which she very probably was, "that he'll cheat you out of the money. He'll find some way to not have to pay you. You're wasting your time."

"Well, we'll just have to make him pay," the gap-toothed man said, waggling the guns in his hand dramatically.

"You two? Against his army of security? Please. You'll be full of holes before you can get your guns drawn."

"That's what you think," the big man holding her said. "I'm the fastest gun this side of the Mississippi. Besides, I have it on good authority that your father is a reliable businessman when it comes to his contracts."

Despite his size and traveling companion, his words didn't sound slow or thick. They sounded calculating and confident. She was in a lot more trouble than she'd first thought, she realized.

"He's taken out other contracts?" she asked, suddenly surprised. Both men chuckled.

"Absolutely," the big man behind her said. "Now, you're going to be a good girl and hold still while I tie you up, aren't you?" She hesitated, and the gap-toothed fellow grinned and cocked the hammer on Hound's gun. Evie nodded.

The big man proceeded to tie her up, quite as effectively as Jack had, though much more painfully. She didn't complain, though. It wouldn't have done her any good.

Once she was securely tied, the big man hoisted her across Patriot's back and led the horse past the next clump of trees, where the two bounty hunters had horses of their own waiting.

Making sure she was lashed down securely, the two men mounted and began heading west again. She bounced and jostled painfully as Patriot trotted to keep up.

Desperately, she wished she had some way to mark her trail so Jack could find her. Odd that she'd been so angry with him, so desperate to be away from him, but now suddenly found herself wishing for nothing more than for him to appear.

It didn't matter, she knew. Whether these two swine had her or Jack did, both would do the same thing; turn her in to her father, collect the money, and ride away.

Evie gave up trying to keep her head up and dropped it down to the side of the saddle. It took only minutes before her light-headedness got the better of her and she passed out.

Evie awoke to the sounds of men talking. Frowning, she took a minute to take stock of her surroundings. It was dark out. She must have been out for hours. She was also lying tied uncomfortably on the ground, rather than across Patriot's back.

Opening her eyes, she could see they were sitting in a small copse of trees, with the railway visible not far beyond. Her two captors sat a few feet away, around a small fire.

The two voices, which she now recognized as the gap-toothed man and his over-sized partner, were suddenly interrupted by a third voice.

"Gentlemen," came the voice from the trees. The voice caused her heart to leap, her stomach to sink, and her eyes to promptly threaten to begin watering again.

Looking toward the voice, she saw him. Jack rode calmly up to the three of them on a brown mare she didn't recognize, stopping some distance out from the fire. Evie turned her eyes to her two captors, terrified they might draw their guns and shoot him down.

They didn't, though. To her surprise, the two men both visibly paled and grew very still.

"Hannity," the big man said, his voice filled with wariness.

"Dayton," Jack replied with a nod. "Regis," he added as he nodded at the second man.

"My God, Jack… What are you doing here?" the big man, Dayton, said.

"I've come to collect my collar and my horse," he said, not looking at Evie.

"Your…" Regis said, confused. Dayton looked over to Patriot where she was tether to a tree.

"Your collar stole your horse?" Dayton said, looking like he wanted to laugh, but a quick glance back at Jack stilled any mirth he might have had.

Evie was stunned. Two brutal bounty hunters like these two were afraid of Jack, even though they outnumbered him. Her estimation of how dangerous Jack was went up a few more notches. She noticed both men were extremely careful not to make any moves that might be construed as being toward their guns.

Jack's coat was drawn back behind the grip of his pistol, leaving it exposed and within easy grip, and she knew he could have it out in a blink if he chose to. His fingers twitched. Dayton and Regis saw it, too. Evie could tell by the way they both flinched.

Jack's eyes never left the two men.

"Come on, now, Jack," Dayton said. "You can take the horse and her bags, but we caught this collar fair and square. Mr. Delano offered us the contract perfectly legal."

"I had her first," Jack clarified. "Picked her up all the way up in Falls City. She was stolen from me, along with my horse, and after dealing with the men involved, I've come to take them both back."

"We need this collar, Jack," Regis whined pathetically. "We ain't been fed proper in a full month!"

"Sounds like you need a new career," Jack said, his half-smile cold and menacing.

"Now, Jack," Dayton started to say, his tone threatening. Jack's fingers twitched, and both men flinched again. Dayton shut his mouth.

"Now, nothing," Jack said. "I'm taking the girl and my horse either way. Only question is whether

I spend two bullets to do it. Cost me three cents, I reckon."

His tone and manner terrified Evie. This, before her now, was the cold killer he'd once been. Jack's deep, smooth voice spoke of killing these men as though it meant no more to him than the cost of a pair of bullets. His steely-gray eyes were as cold as ice, his gaze piercing and hawklike, his powerful body tensed like a coiled cat, ready to make his kill.

Sitting atop the back of the dark horse, coat drawn back, hat brim low, eyes sharp and focused like that, hand ready less than an inch from his gun, he was more menacing than the most deadly outlaws she had ever seen on wanted posters. Those were the men Jack bested for a living, after all.

This was a man to be feared, and these two knew it.

"All… all right, Jack. No need to go that far," Dayton said slowly, his tone obviously intended to be placating.

"Dayton," Regis whined.

"Shut it, Regis," Dayton snapped. "Want us to cut her loose, first?"

"No," Jack said, to her surprise. "This one'll rabbit the moment she's given the chance. Just put her over the horse and untether the mare."

"What are we supposed to do?" Regis whined again. "I'm hungry, Jack!"

"Here," Jack said, left hand moving back to the saddlebags and coming out with an apple. He tossed it to Regis, who looked at it in disgust. "For old times' sake," he added with a mirthless smile.

Dayton had stood and walked over to her. She cringed as he touched her, but he just roughly hoisted her up and walked her over to Patriot. He slung her over the mare's back, and untied the horse's reins. Dayton walked Patriot over to Jack, and held up the reins.

Jack reached down for them, and Dayton moved like a snake. He had his gun drawn, aimed, and pulled the trigger before Evie could call out a warning.

She didn't need to. Jack's gun appeared in his hand pointed at Dayton's eye, coming to a cold stop an inch away. His other hand had flashed out, gripping the top of Dayton's gun, his finger wrapped around between the hammer and the firing pin. The hammer snapped down on Jack's finger, rather than the firing pin, but Jack didn't so much as wince.

Dayton's eyes went wide and rather crossed as they tried to focus on the barrel of Jack's revolver an inch from his eye. Regis cursed slowly, his tone filled with awe.

"Dayton," Jack snarled through clenched teeth, "the only reason I don't let some air into that thick skull of yours right now is on account of you saving my life that once on the Pony Express job. Right this very moment, I consider that account paid in full. Anything you do from this instant on is the start of a new slate between us, do you and I have an understanding?"

Dayton nodded slowly. Jack's gun didn't move, as still as if held by a statue.

"Good man. Now, let go of the revolver and go sit down by your partner and tell him to shuck iron and toss it into the bushes over there. If either of you draws down on me again, or tries to take my collar from me, I'll aim for your yellow belly and spit in the wound. Go on, now. Git."

Dayton backed away slowly, leaving his own revolver in Jack's hand. Jack's eyes, and gun, followed the man until he sat. At a hissed word from Dayton, Regis slowly eased his gun out and tossed it into the bushes where Jack had indicated. Jack nodded once, then holstered his gun and turned his horse away.

"Stay there for a spell, unless you'd care to have dinner tonight with the Lord Almighty," Jack called over his shoulder.

He turned and rode away from the brush. Patriot followed dutifully behind, as Jack led her out of the trees into open ground once more, where he turned and followed the railway.

They'd ridden like that, Jack leading Patriot with Evie across her back, for several minutes before Jack stopped.

She was getting light-headed again, and was relieved he was stopping to cut her loose. He dismounted the brown mare and came back to her.

Lifting her up from her prone position, he shifted her around and moved her up again toward the brown mare.

"What are you doing?" she asked, her tone showing that she was still angry with him.

"Saving your life," he replied coolly.

"Those two coots weren't going to kill me. Just turn me over to my father, same as you."

"Those two coots would have gotten you killed. There are four more men back there about an hour behind me, who had four more friends before I met them, all of which would love nothing better than to put a few holes in you to irritate your father."

Evie was quiet a long moment, thinking about this. He'd saved her life. Again. After she'd stolen his horse and gun. Again. He set her up on the horse, clearly not intending to cut her bonds.

"What are you doing?" she asked again, this time in shrill panic.

"Keeping you tied. I can't trust you," he told her as he began tethering her down. It would keep her upright, but with nearly no room to move.

"Of course you can trust me!" she replied in irritation.

"I've heard that before. And every time, you nearly get me, and your own fool self, killed. Only way to protect you is to let your pa put you under lock and key."

"You're going to keep me tied?" she asked in astonishment and growing outrage. She shouldn't have been surprised, but somehow she was.

"I'd sooner release an angry fox in my britches than cut you loose right now," he replied.

"Untie me, Mr. Hannity!" she yelled.

"Jack," he replied, giving her a cold stare.

"We're not that friendly!" she practically screamed at him.

Jack turned away and moved toward Patriot. He spoke so softly under his breath that she didn't think he'd meant for her to hear. She heard the words, however, and they all but tore her heart from her chest.

"I thought we were, once."

Chapter Fifteen

Evie tried a couple of times to speak, but the jostling against the hard leather saddle kept knocking her about as Jack kept the horses at a steady canter. It was amazing how much more difficult it was to ride upright when you weren't straddling the animal for balance and stability, she thought.

Idly, she wondered if Jack transported many prisoners this way, but remembered he'd told her he usually bound them and dragged them behind the horse if they couldn't walk fast enough. This wasn't comfortable, but it sure beat being dragged behind a horse.

The canter was covering ground quickly, and save for a few brief walking breaks, Jack kept it up consistently. It was becoming increasingly obvious to Evie that he intended to ride straight through and deliver her immediately to her father. It wouldn't be long, she knew, but she had no idea how long it would actually take to get there. No way but to ask, she thought to herself.

The next time Jack slowed the horses to a walk, she took the opportunity.

"How long?"

"Another hour, give or take," was his emotionless reply. He didn't even look back at her. She was angry at him, she reminded herself as she felt a pang of guilt at his coolness.

"I hope you're happy," she said, deciding to take this opportunity to try and make him feel guilty instead. It might make her feel less guilty herself.

"Happy as I ever am," he replied.

"I'll probably be married off to some ridiculously old politician, who likes to beat his women."

"Possible," came his disinterested answer.

Her anger flared again. Didn't he care at all? What had the night before at the hotel been about, then? He had to have been playing her, she thought. There was simply no way he had truly cared that much then only to care so little now. He spoke again, his words confusing her once more.

"Might be that you'll be paired off with a wealthy young buck who'll treat you like a queen, though."

Was that even a possibility? She suddenly found herself wondering, until she actually pictured it. She couldn't fight back the knot in her stomach, and for a moment she wasn't sure why that possibility bothered her.

Because he wouldn't be Jack, she realized, the

knot turning into a sinking pit. Whether he wanted her or not didn't matter, not as far as her feelings for him were concerned. She was angry with him, and hurt, but she loved him.

The idea of marrying anyone other than Jack just felt so horribly wrong she couldn't begin to put it into words. Not that she'd ever speak them anyway. He was delivering her to her father, as he'd promised.

In a day or two, she'd find an opportunity to escape again, and would run. She'd catch a train back up to Falls City, or near enough, and go back to her saloon. She'd have to sell it, and quickly, to have the money to keep running.

Evie had no idea how long her father and his cronies, or his enemies, would be after her, but she was certain she could outrun them. She'd just have to get a train going as far away as she possibly could. Then, she'd open another saloon, and start over.

Without Jack.

She tried to fight back her tears as she thought of a future without him, but failed. Quietly, she instructed herself as a sort of compromise. She couldn't let him know she was crying. She wouldn't give him the satisfaction.

He had to have had feelings for her, though. The warmth in his eyes when they woken in each other's arms had been unmistakable. So what was it now? Why was he so determined to complete this contract?

He'd implied more than once that he didn't really need the money. She wasn't a criminal, so it wasn't his vigilante sense of justice. It couldn't just be his word, either. He was a man of integrity, but she was sure that if he thought it was in her best interest for him to break his word, he would. It had to be what he'd said before, that her father could protect her better than anyone else.

Why couldn't he understand that she was nothing more than an asset to her father? He'd protect her, sure, right up until the moment he handed her off for marriage to some other man. At which point, he'd get some political favor owed to him, and his asset would be spent, and no longer his concern.

In fairness, once she no longer 'belonged' to her father, she wouldn't be much of a target to his enemies anymore, so there was that. It wasn't worth it, though. That much she never questioned. No amount of protection was worth sacrificing her freedom. Anyone who thought otherwise was a plumb fool, no mistake.

The thought crossed her mind that she should ask Jack to just run with her, but she knew it wouldn't work. She'd tried it already, and he'd turned her down flat.

He was convinced her father was the best person to protect her, and so that was where he would take her. They rode hard now not because he wished to be rid of her as quickly as possible, or at least not only because of that, but because he'd said there were men not far behind him who were after her, and he wasn't willing to risk stopping.

"We could run," she said, totally involuntarily. Jack almost looked back, his head turning slightly.

"They'd find you," he replied.

He'd said 'you', not 'us', she noted painfully. Jack probably did want to be rid of her, though. After all, she'd almost gotten him killed several times, stolen his horse and gun more than once, had forced a reunion with someone he'd avoided for years, and while that had turned out well, who knew whether he resented her at all for it.

"We could go too far for them to find us," she replied, hating how pleading her tone sounded.

"Who knows how many of them we'd have to fight off to make it that far. In less than a hundred miles, we've been attacked four times. No, Evie, we need to get you someplace safe. Running isn't the right move."

"My father will only protect me until he can marry me off," she spat.

"At which point, you'll still be safe."

"Maybe not from my husband," she flung back, bitterly. Evie could see his shoulders move as he took a long, slow breath.

"It's better than getting shot at every other day."

Evie wasn't at all sure that it was.

This couldn't be over soon enough, Jack thought. His heart was raging at him, guilt, longing, and hopelessness tearing at him from the inside.

Evie's words didn't help. She had rather sharply reminded him what price she'd potentially be paying for her safety. No, she'd never sit still and cooperate long enough for that to happen, he thought for the thousandth time.

Except that meant she'd be running out loose and alone, unprotected, while she went back to her saloon. She'd go there first, he knew, and anyone else after her would know that, too. She was a bright gal, but when it came to a life like his, she had no idea.

Jack bit back a growl of frustration. He couldn't protect her forever. Hell, he had barely protected her for three days, and much of that was luck. There were too many people looking for her, bounty hunter and hired killer alike. One man simply couldn't keep her safe.

Unless that man had a lot of money, like her father. His security team was decent, making up in numbers what they lacked in skill, and would be able to keep her under a watchful eye. She wouldn't be able to escape.

Which meant she'd be forced into marriage with someone who might be worse than her father.

Jack cursed under his breath. What kind of choices was he being left with?

He could run with her. They'd be together, for however long it took for someone to fnd and eventually kill her.

He could turn her over to her father. She'd be protected, until she was forced into a marriage that might be worse than death.

Or he could turn her over to her father, and she'd escape, leaving herself unprotected and alone, and more than likely dead within a day.

Turning her over to her father was the only chance she had to not end up dead in less than a week. Her father might not even be planning to marry her off, and even if he did, the odds she'd end up with someone that terrible was incredibly slim.

Evie might even end up with a man who'd love her the way she deserved. It was her best chance, even if she hated him for it. Jack hated himself for it, so that was perfectly reasonable.

He had no choice. He hadn't ever had a choice.

His thoughts turned forcibly to the steady rhythm of the horses' canter. Jack could drone out a full day's riding that way without getting too lost in his own thoughts. He only had a short time left, he could do this.

After what felt an impossibly long time, Topeka was ahead and he could see the lanterns shining. He ached to turn around and look at her, but he was afraid if he did, he'd break and set her free, running off into the distance with her. Where she would die. He kept his eyes locked forward.

They rode into the city, heading for the lieutenant governor's mansion. It was late, or rather early, so there weren't many folk around, but it was a big city so there was always someone about. Every eye turned his way, eyeing Evie tied behind him.

Jack suffered a pang of guilt for her dignity, but she'd never come willingly. She had made that abundantly clear. If he had to hogtie her and sling her belly-first over the mare's back to take her where she'd be safe, he'd do it.

Someday, he prayed, someday she may forgive me. Not likely, his more realistic side retorted, but she'd be alive.

Evie didn't say another word the whole ride. Jack half expected a sharp remark as they approached the gate to her father's estate, but she was silent. He wasn't sure if that was better or worse than the alternative.

As they approached the gate, a trio of hired guards stepped forward to stop him. Three gate guards? Mr. Delano must have really angered some folk, Jack thought. He was right in the middle of town, it wasn't as if a band of killers could just charge in and murder him and ride back out.

"Evening," Jack said with a touch to his hat.

"Morning," one of the men corrected. Jack nodded his acceptance.

"Morning it is," he accepted. "I'm here for Mr.

Delano. I've got his daughter here, as promised."

The men looked behind Jack to Evie, and one of them snickered at her bound condition. Jack gave him a dark look, and the smile slid from his face.

"Go let the man know I've brought his daughter, sir, I ain't got all night."

"I don't take orders from…" he began, but Jack interrupted.

"Mr. Delano will be most annoyed if he learns he was not immediately informed of his precious daughter's arrival, don't you think? If it's worth five hundred dollars to him to have her returned promptly, it's certainly worth your job."

The man glared at him, but Jack's cold stare caused the guard to look away after only a few seconds. Nodding, the man turned and went through the gate toward the huge house.

The waiting seemed to go on forever as he sat Patriot's back in front of her father's home. This was it, he knew. In a few minutes, she'd be in her father's hands, and Jack himself would be back on the road. Evie wouldn't say goodbye to him, he was sure. She was too angry, and rightfully so.

The guard finally came back out and opened the gate.

"Mr. Delano will see you in his study. The butler will show you the way."

Jack tipped his hat to the men and rode through the open gate, leading the brown mare with Evie on her back. They rode to the front of the house, where a stableboy waited to take their reins. Jack dismounted and went back to untie Evie. Just enough to get her off the horse, anyway.

"I'm sorry," he said softly.

Evie didn't respond. Jack couldn't blame her. He briefly considered carrying her in his arms, but decided that would imply too much, to both her and her father, so he slung her over his shoulder.

Evie didn't make a sound, but he could feel her seething. Jack sighed and went up the steps, where the butler was waiting.

"This way, sir," the older gentleman said. Jack nodded and followed him into the house.

Jack knew the way, since this was where he'd met with Mr. Delano in the first place to get the contract, but he followed the slow-moving butler anyway. Reaching the study, he nodded his thanks at the butler and entered the room.

Mr. Delano sat in his over-sized, brown leather wingback chair behind his huge desk, wrapped in a red velvet formal robe that did nothing for his portly figure. With his red, veined face that told Jack he'd had a drink or two before Jack had walked in, he looked very much like a huge, crimson toad squatting in the mud.

Another man, in a suit and holding a cigar between his teeth despite the hour, stood nearby. A bodyguard, Jack immediately recognized. He knew the type, though he was a different man than Mr. Delano had guarding him a week ago.

Her father saw Evie trussed up over Jack's shoulder and smiled in a most self-satisfied way. Seeing him now through Evie's eyes, Jack completely understood Evie's dislike of the man.

"Mr…" Mr. Delano started, drawing it out and raising a brow to indicate he didn't recall Jack's name.

"Hannity," Jack reminded him. The man waved a hand dismissively, as if it didn't really matter.

"I see you've returned my daughter," he said casually. Jack set Evie down on her own two feet, keeping a hand on her shoulder to steady her, then eased her into one of the chairs on this side of the desk.

"Yes, sir," Jack responded, keeping his tone respectful despite his desire to punch the man right in his fat second chin.

"She appears well," he said. Jack risked a glance, but Evie's death gaze was focused tightly on her father.

"Yes, sir," he replied.

"Good to see you, Evelyn, dear," he said, finally addressing his daughter.

"How could you," she snarled, voice barely above a whisper.

"Didn't Mr… umm… Hannity tell you? This was for your protection. You should have come along peacefully, but I can see our friend here had to take extreme measures to bring you home."

"This isn't my home," she snapped. "It hasn't

been since Mother died."

Mr. Delano's expression darkened, but he turned to Jack instead.

"Well, Mr. Hannity, I have to apologize, but the bounty was cancelled." Jack's heart iced as his blood instantly began to boil.

"Pardon?" he asked. Mr. Delano leaned forward slightly and spoke slowly, as if Jack were a bit thick.

"The bounty contract. It was terminated yesterday. You see, the men I was having trouble with came to an agreement with me, so my daughter is no longer in danger. As such, the bounty has been discontinued. I'm afraid delivering her here isn't worth a penny. It was publicly posted, as required. You didn't see it, riding in?"

Jack felt a surge of rage flood through him. The man was actually going to try and cheat him. This bounty wasn't about the money, but Jack wasn't about to let this fat toad get away with trying to cheat him. It was bad enough he had Evie again.

He took a half step forward, and eased back the side of his long coat, just barely exposing his gun. The suited man shifted stance slightly, moving his own gun slightly into view. Jack tracked the man's movements peripherally, but didn't take his eyes off of Mr. Delano.

"Sir, I've gone through hell bringing this gal here, under fair and legal contract with you. I've completed my end of the signed contract, and you're going to complete yours, or we'll have ourselves a bit of a fuss."

"You're welcome to pursue legal action, Mr. Hannity, but you'll see I've followed all proper legal procedures. The contract is null and void."

"Oh, it won't come to that, Mr. Delano. I killed more than a dozen men on the way down here who were looking to do your daughter harm. You're about two shakes of a lamb's tail from finding out why my name makes dangerous men all across this fine country go pale at the sound of it."

Mr. Delano paled himself, but glanced at the man to the side.

"My bodyguard…" he began, voice shaky.

"Dies a quarter second before you do," Jack informed him, tone icy. "Five hundred, as agreed, and we can all walk away from this."

The fat man stared at him, but had trouble holding Jack's hawk-like gaze. After a moment that stretched painfully long for everyone in the room, Mr. Delano nodded.

"Mr. Puckett, please retrieve Mr. Hannity's money," he said.

Jack's stance eased, but only slightly, as the bodyguard, Mr. Puckett, went to a safe on the wall, and came back a few moments later with a bound stack of bills. He handed them to Jack, who gave them a quick look. Once sure they weren't trying to cheat him again, he nodded.

"Thank you, Mr. Delano. Please hesitate to

contact me again in the future if you have further need of my talents."

He didn't offer his hand, and neither did Warren Delano. Jack looked down at Evie, who was still glaring fiercely at her father. For a moment, he thought the anger at her father had eclipsed her anger for him, but as he watched her, he saw her eyes tighten slightly as she pointedly ignored his gaze. He tipped his hat to her, then to the two men.

"Ma'am. Gentlemen." With that, he turned on his heel and swept out of the room.

Chapter Sixteen

Evie couldn't seem to stop crying. Every time she thought she'd managed to get control of it, an errant thought of Jack would brush her mind and the whole house of cards came crashing down again.

She had managed to sleep a little after her father had Mr. Puckett carry her up to her room before cutting her free, then closing and locking her bedroom door. Evie had barely made it to the bed before her knees gave out and she'd cried herself to sleep.

The fact that her father had kept her room exactly as she'd left it wasn't surprising. He still considered her his, and needed to keep the place ready for the time he was ready to collect his property again.

Evie had even taken a look at the window during one of her brief moments of control, where her anger overran her despair. She'd been hoping it might make a good escape route, but there were two guards posted below it, some distance out, and facing her. There would be no escape that way, unless they both fell asleep on the job.

There had to be an opportunity, she told herself. She just had to be on the lookout for it. Jack would know what to do, she thought. And then she broke down again.

Did it matter, she thought, if she escaped or not? Alone and on the run, or forced into a marriage she didn't want, her life would never be hers. Jack would never be hers.

Some hours later, after the sun had risen, there was a knock at the door. Before she could do more than climb out of bed, the door opened. Mr. Puckett was there, holding a tray of food. He moved into the room without acknowledging her, and went to set the tray on the small writing desk.

Evie bolted for the door. Certain she'd made it as her fingers touched the doorknob, Mr. Puckett's strong hands grabbed her and slung her back into the room. She fell backwards, landing hard on her back, knocking the wind out of her.

"Don't even try it, Evelyn," he'd sneered.

"Miss Delano," she gasped back, trying to sound as angry as she felt, and assert some authority as a member of the Delano family. He ignored it.

"Stunts like that will just get you hurt, and I ain't playing around," he told her, before leaving the room and locking the door behind himself.

It had been hours before her father had finally deigned to come see her. He walked in, Mr. Puckett behind him, and smiled at her. Mr. Puckett took up a post beside the door. She shook her head in disgust. Her own father felt he needed a bodyguard to protect him from her. He did, but that wasn't the point, she thought angrily.

"Good morning, my dear," he said.

"I'm not your 'dear'," she threw back.

"You'll always be my little girl, Evelyn," he replied. His voice had taken on that patronizing, insulting tone he always used on the rare occasion that he spoke to her as a child.

"So, who is it?" she asked him.

"Who is what?" he replied, confused.

"The man you're going to wed me off to. The only reason you'd pay five hundred dollars to get me back is because you need me. It sure wasn't for my protection, except to protect a valuable piece of property, so don't give me any of that rubbish."

"I'm hurt that you don't think your safety means the world to me. Of course it was for your protection!" He had put on his 'wounded' face. She had seen that one too often as he manipulated people to buy it for even a second.

"Who is it?" she asked again, firmly. He took a deep breath, then sighed.

"Sheriff Dickerson's son is a fine young man. They have some money, and you'll live comfortably."

She made a sound of disgust in the back of her throat.

"So you'll have a back door with the sheriff

when you need legal help, or legal ignorance? Does Caleb know about this?" she asked.

Caleb was the sheriff's son. He was a decent boy, from what she'd seen in years past. Of course, that was some time ago. It could have been worse, though. Much worse.

"Nonsense, Evelyn," her father replied. "He's asked for your hand, and his father and I simply think it's a good match. I told him you had left some years back, but when the ruckus about the coal mine came up, I knew I had to get you back for your safety. This simply works out as convenient timing for everyone that Caleb has just returned from college with his law degree."

"Ah, I see," she said in exaggerated tones. "A sheriff *and* a lawyer. Two birds with one stone, that's quite efficient. I'm impressed."

"Evelyn, I'm getting tired of your tone," her father said, threateningly. "The Dickersons are coming for dinner this evening, and I expect you to be on your best behavior."

"Or what?" she asked.

What could he possibly do to her that was worse than he was already doing? His expression turned dark and malicious, and she unexpectedly found herself staring into the eyes of the man who had beaten her mother to within an inch of her life many, many times. She involuntarily leaned back.

"Or you'll learn the lesson your mother had such a hard time learning. I am to be obeyed,

Evelyn. Disobedience is unacceptable, and will be punished. Am I clear?"

Evie had no choice. She nodded. Her father used to have a doctor on the payroll just to covertly treat her mother on the nights her father decided she needed to be put 'in her place'. Evie knew exactly how bad it could get, and not for the first time, found herself envying her mother dying and getting free of this man.

Her father had never beaten her. He'd never needed to, since Evelyn had only to see what 'punishments' he dished out to her mother to fall sharply into line. Evie suspected her mother had protected her a great deal, as well.

She'd seen that look in his eyes before, though, and knew that what would follow for her was every bit as bad, and she'd have the opportunity to find out if her father still had Doc Hutchins in his pocket.

He gave her his most menacing glare, then stood and headed for the door.

"Wear the green dress," he ordered sharply. "It sets off your eyes." With that, the two men left, slamming and locking the door behind them.

Evie sat across from Caleb Dickerson, who had been polite, but kept eyeing her in a manner that told her that his interest wasn't exclusively a romantic one. It was a shame, seeing a boy she'd always considered to be nice enough having bought into the nonsense his father no doubt kept feeding him about a woman's 'place'.

She'd considered refusing coming down for dinner altogether, but she wouldn't be in any physical condition to try to escape after her father got through with her for her disobedience. Evie had even worn the green dress, and hated herself for it.

Despite her attendance, she couldn't help but wonder if maybe her presence hadn't been necessary at all. She had spoken perhaps a dozen words the entire meal, while the sheriff, his son, and her father, casually discussed her future and her marriage.

Again, she'd been tempted to tell everyone exactly what she thought of this whole mess, but she kept reminding herself how she needed to be strong and healthy to escape when her opportunity came.

"What do you think, Evelyn?" came her father's question. Being addressed surprised her nearly as much as the fact that he was actually asking her opinion on anything.

"I beg your pardon?" she asked, knowing it would annoy her father that she hadn't been paying attention, but not having any choice but to ask at this point.

"I said," he replied with a warning tone, "do you prefer white roses or peach for your wedding bouquet? Women," he said, giving a long-suffering look to the two men, "this is why they don't belong in politics."

The three men laughed, though Caleb had at least enough decency to give her an embarrassed look. He wasn't all bad, he just didn't stand much of a chance against the sheer force of his father, and now hers, pushing against him.

He was still a boy, she thought. He'd never been allowed to grow into his own man, though he was her age. Even Caleb's pursuit of his law degree had been his father's decision, not his own. What a waste, she thought. Jack would never have allowed himself to be railroaded like that. The thought of him set a lump firmly in her throat.

"Evelyn?" her father interrupted her thoughts again. She barely restrained a flinch at his tone.

"Oh, I think whatever you decide will be just fine," she said, knowing it was what he wanted to hear.

He smiled his contentment with that reply, and nodded.

"White it is, then," he told the sheriff, who nodded as if her father's decision were some profound and wise one. Evie barely kept from rolling her eyes in disgust.

Poking at the chicken on her plate, her thoughts involuntarily went back to Jack. She wondered where he'd gone. It had been nearly a full day since he had left her here, an act she kept telling herself was an ultimate betrayal.

Part of her understood him, though. She knew

why he'd done it, whether she agreed with the decision or not. He'd wanted to protect her. Enough to tie her up and deliver her to a horrible man who would use her, as he used everything else in his life.

Jack couldn't know how terrible her father was, though. All he knew was that she was being hunted, and her father's battalion of hired private security was the best possible protection.

Except she didn't need protection now, since her father had already told them both that the problem had been resolved. Her father had probably had the leader of the group standing against him killed. In any case, the only thing she needed protection from now was her father, and she wished Jack could understand that.

She started to sigh, but bit it back as she remembered she wasn't alone. Caleb caught it, though, and glanced at her questioningly. He looked genuinely concerned, which made her soften toward him a little more.

The sheriff's son probably wouldn't be a terrible husband. He'd never been cruel, and while he was obviously quite interested in how she filled out her bodice, he had been embarrassed by her father's attitudes even though he hadn't actually stood up for her, and now looked at her with what appeared genuine concern.

For the briefest moment, she felt a bit guilty that she was going to escape and leave him abandoned. Only for a moment, though. He'd find someone who shared his interest. He was a handsome man, and generally a kind person. In all honesty, he might not even realize she was being forced into this.

Evie only hoped he managed to break free of his father's control, so he could someday enjoy some happiness of his own. That would be his problem, however, not hers. Her only problem right now was figuring out how to escape from her own father's iron grip.

She smiled back at him reassuringly, and he nodded once, looking mostly satisfied by the response. The last thing she needed right now was him realizing there was a problem and bringing it up to his father.

A servant came and cleared the dinner plates, and brought dessert. Evie did sigh this time, regretting not eating the chicken. She'd need her strength, and wasn't sure how long it would be once she got out onto the trail before she'd be able to get ahold of substantial food again.

Evie had nothing by way of trail gear. She did have her riding clothes, the ones she'd tricked Jack into buying for her, but that was it. She had no money, no supplies, no food, no horse, nothing.

"Evelyn?" her father asked. She mentally cursed herself for letting that sigh escape. She realized all three men were regarding her with various levels of concern.

"I'm sorry," she said with a small smile. "I was

just thinking this would be my last dessert for a while. I don't want to appear unsightly in my wedding dress, after all."

"Well, we certainly wouldn't want that," her father said, eyes dark. He waved, and a servant came and took the untouched dish away. Evie grit her teeth. "There. No time like the present to start," he told her with a smirk.

"No time, indeed," she answered, forcing a smile.

"Come now," Caleb said, "no reason to be concerned about that, Miss Delano. You look quite lovely, and I daresay it would take quite a few more tarts than that one to damage your fine figure in the least. This is a happy occasion, and one certainly worth a bit of indulgence." He waved at the servant, who had hesitated at his interruption.

The servant glanced at her father questioningly. After an uncomfortably long pause, he nodded, and the servant brought the tart back to her. She gave Caleb a grateful look, and he smiled. Well, she owed the man one, then.

Not one marriage, of course, but a small debt of gratitude at any rate. She'd send him an apology by post when she'd made it back to her saloon, she decided. He deserved that much, since she'd come to the conclusion that he didn't know she was being forced into this arrangement.

Her father looked unhappy, which inspired her to vindictively make a show of pleasure as she took a delicate bite of the pastry. His scowl darkened, and she gave him a smile. He'd probably only hit her once for that. Entirely worth it.

Evie only wished she could see his face when he realized she was gone in the morning.

Chapter Seventeen

Evie had bid the Dickersons good evening and gone to bed when the men had decided to adjourn to the study for some brandy and cigars.

She had no intention of actually going to bed, of course. Mr. Puckett had escorted her to her room and locked the door, as she expected. Waiting was the hardest part.

Pacing her room, unable to rest, she kept glancing out the window. She had to wait long enough that she was sure nobody was still up in the hallway. It had been silent for quite some time, but she wasn't quite ready, yet.

The two men outside her window down below glanced up every time she passed. They were attentive, she'd give them that much.

What would happen if she were caught, she wondered? She wouldn't be, she replied fiercely, shoving the doubts away. Every time she thought of getting caught, that lump rose in her throat and she felt tears threatening.

There would be plenty of time to break down

after she'd saved herself, she told herself sternly. For now, she needed to be strong and focused.

A few minutes before she felt the time had come, she moved to her wardrobe and pulled out the riding clothes she'd hidden in the back.

Changing quickly, she fought hard to keep her breath and heartbeat steady. She needed to be cool as ice, like Jack. If only Jack were here, she thought. He'd know right away if her plan would work. He wasn't here, she reminded herself. Jack was probably thirty miles out of town already. He'd had a full day's ride since dropping her into her father's lap, and wouldn't have wasted any time getting clear with his money.

What he would do with the money, she had no idea. He probably had quite a lot saved. He seemed like the type to be smart, and his lifestyle was very inexpensive. The money had to go someplace. Not that it was any of her business, she thought.

He certainly wouldn't retire, though. Jack would keep hunting bounties until he died, of that she was sure. Which didn't seem likely any time soon, despite his extremely dangerous career. Evie had never met a man so capable of handling himself when things got rough. She had never felt safer than when he was right there with her.

Sighing again, she pushed down the threatening tears and shook her thoughts free. She tied her hair back, removing the fancy style she'd arranged to go with the green dress. She kept a hairpin handy, though. Evie moved to her bedroom door.

Pressing an ear against it, she listened intently. Across the house, she could just make out the occasional laughter of the men in the study below, but she heard nothing in the hallway. Kneeling down, she peered through the keyhole.

Perfect, she thought with a feeling of victory, small one though it may be. The key was still in the keyhole on the far side. Mr. Puckett should be smarter than that, she thought. Evie was glad he wasn't, but a professional of his pay rate should be smarter.

Quickly, she moved to her small writing desk, and drew out a sheet of paper. Heading back to the door, she slid the sheet beneath it, keeping just enough on her side to be able to pull it back. She got into a semi-comfortable kneeling position on the floor in front of the doorknob.

Pulling out the hairpin again, she slid it into the lock, pushing on the key. Grumbling, she realized it was still turned and wouldn't easily slide out. Wiggling the pin, she tried to angle it into the hole to catch the edge of the key, trying to pull it down. The pin kept slipping off.

With a soft curse, the pulled the pin out, and placed the tip between her teeth. Carefully, she bent the tip slighty. Going back into the lock with the pin, she once more tried to hook the key. The pin felt like it was getting a better hold on the key, but it still wouldn't turn.

Once more, she pulled the pin out and bent it a bit further. A few more moments, and she felt the pin hook securely on the key. Twisting it down, she felt the key rotate slightly before the pin slipped again. Another attempt, and she felt the key turn the rest of the way. It was aligned with the keyhole on the other side now, she just needed to… there!

She held her breath in simultaneous panic and excitement as the key fell out of the keyhole on the far side, falling to the ground with a loud *CLINK*.

Waiting for what felt an eternity, she listened for anyone who might come to investigate the sound. Nobody came. Releasing the breath slowly, she reached down and took hold of the narrow edge of paper still visible beneath the door.

Sliding it slowly back inside the room, she felt her heartbeat pounding. If this didn't work, she didn't know what she'd do. There it was! She almost whooped in relief. The key lay there, right on the edge of the piece of paper. As she pulled the paper in, the key came with it. Grinning broadly, she put the key in the lock.

The lamplight flickered behind her, casting odd shadows of herself on the door and wall above it. The shapes looked peculiar, she thought, pausing in her work. The shadows looked larger than they should be, and were moving strangely. Evie had an odd sense of déjà vu. She stood very slowly. The shadows had stopped moving.

Someone was in her room. It couldn't be, she

thought. It wasn't possible. But if it wasn't him…

She stood tall and straight, ready to fight as she turned around. Right in front of her eyes was a broad chest in a sage green shirt.

Her heart froze as her eyes slid disbelievingly up into the slate-gray eyes above and she gasped in a breath. The piercing gaze that regarded her was sparkling with mischief, but the expression on the handsome, stubbled face was one of uncertainty.

"Darlin'," Jack's voice said softly.

"Dear Lord," she breathed, "what are you doing here?"

"Same thing I've been doing all week. Protecting you."

"I don't need your help," she said sharply, desperately fighting the urge to simply leap at him, wrapping her arms around his waist, never to let him go. She was supposed to be angry with him, she reminded herself.

"So I see." Jack glanced at the paper on the floor and the key in the lock and smiled. The expression looked distinctly proud, which made her feel irrationally pleased with herself. "I reckon you had a plan for the two fellas at the bottom of the stairs?"

Her ego promptly deflated. She'd had no idea that her father had stationed two men at the bottom of the stairs.

"I wasn't going out that way," she lied. She actually had intended to, assuming that her safest route was through the kitchens, since it was unlikely her father had posted guards right there. Now she wasn't so sure, if he'd put men at the stairs, too.

"The bedroom across the way is watched from the outside. So's the window at the end of the hall," he told her.

"I'd have figured something out," she said, scowling. Despite her attitude, she was elated that he was here, right in front of her. She ached to touch him, as if she had a need to prove to herself that he really was there.

"I reckon so," he said.

"What are you doing here?" she asked him again, pointedly.

"I told you, protecting you."

"I don't need protection anymore, remember? My father's enemies have come to an agreement with him."

"I meant from your father," he answered. Tears burned at her eyes, but she fought them down. He really had understood.

"What about your precious contract? Your word?" she said, the words having less venom than she'd intended.

Her anger and resentment were melting fast in the face of those eyes. His eyes, his half-smile, his scent, everything about him being here had thrown her anger right out the guarded window.

"Contract's complete," he replied. "Paid in full. I promised your father I'd bring you back here to him, safe and sound. I did so, my word has been honored. I recall telling you some time back that what happened after that was fair game."

Her heart surged. He was really here. Jack had come for her. Not in a thousand lifetimes would she have imagined he would have come back.

"So you come to get me out. Then what?"

"Not rightly sure," he answered. "I seem to recall someone promising me free whiskey at her saloon."

Evie couldn't help it, she grinned.

"You're a boor," she told him. His answering grin filled her with warmth.

"And a ruffian, and a liar, and a thief."

"And sometimes charming," she added. He chuckled.

"Sometimes?"

"Sometimes," she agreed. She wouldn't give him more than that. Not when his grin was so self-satisfied. Her own smile threatened to overwhelm her face.

"Maybe I don't want to go with you," she said suddenly. "You left me here with a man who wanted to sell me into marriage to the sheriff's son."

"That's who those two are?" Jack asked, curiously. She was momentarily surprised.

"Yes, my fiancé and his father," she said sharply. He chuckled again.

"You could do worse," he said.

Evie hesitated, unsure how much of herself to

reveal. His sudden appearance had her head spinning. More than anything, she wanted to tell him she wanted him, not some sheriff's son. She wanted to ride off with him and never look back.

"I could do better," she said instead.

"Sure could," he agreed, without hesitation.

"So what's your plan?" she asked him.

"Out the window, down the roof, onto the trellis, then over the east wall."

"The guards will see us," she argued. He shook his head.

"Not these two. They're… sleeping."

"Jack, you didn't…" she said, both impressed and horrified. It made sense, though. That was how he'd come in, after all. Moving to the window, she couldn't see anyone outside.

"They'll be all right," he clarified, "though they'll both have a headache to reckon with in a few hours."

"The study is below us," she said. "My father and the sheriff will see us coming down the trellis."

"Wrong again. They're out on the west side of the house, by the stables."

"What? Why?" she asked, confused. There was no reason for the men to be out that way. They should be drinking and smoking in the study below.

"Terrible accident with a lantern in the stables. Very unfortunate," he answered, his grin sparkling with mischief.

"Jack, the horses!" she said in horror, starting

to turn toward the door.

"Easy there, darlin'," he replied, catching her shoulder. His touch sent an tingling thrill down her arm, and a warmth to flood her entire body. "You think I'd do something like that? Don't you worry, I let the horses out, first."

As if to punctuate his words, a pair of her father's prized stallions raced past below.

"Jack, you're…" she had no idea what to say. He just grinned.

"I know, I know," he said.

There was a moment of awkwardness as they stood there, each unsure what to say.

"Evie, I'm sorry," he finally said.

"Don't be. You did what you had to do."

"I know, but I don't feel any less sorry for it. Your father is a real piece of work. I wasn't sure I believed you when you said he was going to force you into marriage. What kind of man does that? You haven't even been home a day and he's got your intended over for a nice dinner."

"He is something else," she said darkly. "I don't ever want to lay eyes on him again."

"You won't have to," he assured her. "All right then, so if you don't want to stick with me for a while, and I don't rightly blame you if you don't, here's the deal. I'll get you out of here and to the train station. Where you go from there is up to you."

"I don't have money for a ticket."

"Won't be a problem, your ticket is on your

father," he said, patting a pocket. She laughed.

"I won't refuse that," she replied.

"Of course, if you'd rather," he said, looking uncertain again, "we could ride back to Falls City together. I'd... I'd like to take you home."

"You'd want to do that ride over again? I nearly got you killed, more than once."

"And shot me, and stole my horse, twice," he added, "but there's nowhere I'd rather be than with you, shot at or otherwise. Don't get me wrong, I prefer otherwise, but I'll take it either way, as long as it's with you." His steely eyes had turned warm and soft, his tone the same.

"Why would you want me?" she asked. She genuinely wanted to know, though the words were more an expression of disbelief than anything else.

"Ever since Lucy and the children..." he paused, visibly collecting himself, "I've never felt right. Not once. Something about you makes me feel right. Like everything is normal, only better than normal. Like I can live again. I don't know what will happen between us, things are different when you're not being shot at all the time, but I know I want to find out. I want to try living again, and I want nothing more than to try it with you."

A few tears slipped out, and he reached up quickly to wipe them in a gesture that made them both smile.

"What do you say, Evie? Come with me?"

"Yes," she said, more sincerity in that one word

than she felt sure she'd ever spoken in her life.

His relieved, excited smile made everything, every moment of it all, worth it. The spark of playfulness glinted in his eyes.

"You're going to be trouble, aren't you?" he said accusingly.

"Me? Heavens, no. I'll be on my best behavior, I promise," she said, keeping her face mostly straight. He laughed and shook his head.

"Lord help me," he muttered to the ceiling.

"Someone's got to," she retorted.

"Well, darlin', you about ready to go? Won't be long before good ol' Puckett shows up to check on you, what with all the ruckus going on outside. Got anything to round up?"

"No, I'm wearing everything useful that I own right now. Going to be a long ride both of us on Patriot, again."

"I kept the brown mare for you." For a moment, he looked a touch embarrassed. "I named her Applejack," he admitted.

Evie's cheeks flushed with pleasure at the gesture. It was, undoubtedly, the sweetest thing anyone had ever done with her in mind.

"You really are charming, when you want to be, Mr. Hannity," she told him.

"Jack," he corrected.

"We're not that friendly," she quipped.

"Like hell, we're not," he growled as he grabbed her, pulling her in sharply. His lips met hers fiercely, with an intensity and passion that made the warmth he always brought up in her to flare into a burning heat she had forgotten she was capable of.

Evie pressed her lips back against his, arms going around him as he held her tightly. She felt his tongue brush her lips and she involuntarily let out the barest hint of a moan. As she pushed in harder, he pushed her back and held her at arm's reach. His breath was heavy and throaty, and she could feel her own every bit the same.

"Easy there, darlin'," he told her. "No time for that kind of nonsense. One fire on this property is enough, I think."

"I love you, Jack," she said, without thought. For a moment, he hesitated, stunned.

She was stunned herself, she hadn't intended to say it. It was entirely true, however. She'd known it beyond a shadow of a doubt the instant the words had left her lips. Slowly, as if unsure he could say the words, he replied, his voice deep and rich.

"I love you, too, Evie."

She pushed back towards him, and he let her. Kissing him again, this time she filled it with all the tenderness she felt for him, and he responded in full measure.

When at last she pulled away again, she smiled softly at him. He returned the smile, touched her cheek tenderly, and whispered two words.

"Let's ride."

"I appreciate you looking after my girls while I was gone," Evie said. Ben nodded with a smile.

"My pleasure, Miss Delano. Those girls need someone to keep an eye on them. I'm just glad you're all right."

"Perfectly fine, Ben. I do appreciate the concern, however. Thanks to Jack, it all turned out all right."

Evie looked away from Ben, who stood behind the bar wiping down a mug with a clean rag. Her eyes found Jack, sitting in the same corner he had the day he'd first seen her, or so he'd told her. His long coat brushed the floor as he leaned back in the chair, one leg propped up. His hat was pulled low and he sipped a glass of whiskey. He looked every bit the hardened man he was.

Jack's eyes came up, as if he could feel hers on him. The moment their eyes locked, his warm smile touched his lips, and she again saw the man he was before, and was becoming again. Her eyes found the gold ring on his finger, and her heart swelled.

They had stopped and stayed with his friend Reverend Jarrett for near a month on the way back home. She'd had to send notice to Ben that she wasn't dead. Shortly before they had left, Jack had asked her to marry him. In a few short weeks, she'd fallen more in love with him than she ever had been before. More than she'd ever thought possible. Without a trace of doubt in her mind, she'd said yes.

Reverend Jarrett had performed the ceremony at sunset in the field behind the church, just the three of them, with the sheriff and his deputy as witnesses.

"I'm right glad he found you," Ben said. Evie hadn't told him the full truth, explaining only that her horrible father had sent a bounty hunter after her, and Jack had rescued her.

"So am I," she said softly. "Well," she added, turning back to Ben, "just about finished here." Handing the rolled document in her hand to Ben, he set the mug and rag down, taking the document in one hand, and reaching to shake her hand with the other. "It's all official, then. The saloon is yours."

"I can't thank you enough," he told her sincerely, his big, gruff voice sounding suddenly almost childish with emotion.

"It's my pleasure," she told him. "I'm so glad that you wanted it. I couldn't have sold to just anyone. I needed to know my girls were going to be taken care of. Besides, with your little one on the way…" she said with a smile. His answering grin made him look even more childish in its excitement.

"My son's going to grow up strong and smart, with enough money for an education, thanks to you."

"You sure it'll be a son?" she asked.

"My wife says it will be. I'm not fool enough to argue that. Truth be told, though, I'll be just as thrilled if it turns out to be a little girl."

"Please send me a message when the baby comes. I simply have to come out and meet him. Or her," she laughed. Ben nodded.

"It'd be an honor," Ben replied. "Thank you."

"Take care, Ben."

He set the document down and came around the bar, wrapping her in his big, powerful arms. She hugged him back, choking up at the thought of how much she'd miss him.

Jack came up behind them, sensing she was almost ready to leave. When Ben let her go, he turned to Jack.

"You just keep taking care of Miss Delano, here. She takes a lot of looking after," Ben told him seriously. Jack laughed.

"I know that full well, sir," Jack replied. "Don't you worry. I'll have my eyes on this one every second of every day."

Ben nodded, and the two men shook hands. It seemed a little odd to her that beside Ben, Jack actually looked small. Jack was no small man, but he was a good few inches and an easy hundred pounds smaller than the new owner of the saloon.

Jack stepped outside to get the horses ready, while Evie went to say goodbye to her girls, who had been waiting, most in tears, to see her off.

Evie began to choke up herself, tears threatening to ruin her composure. Her tears were not only for the goodbyes to so many good friends and the life she'd built for herself here with her own two hands. At least a few were in excitement and disbelief at the new life she was building, with Jack.

He had just finished the purchase of a sizeable cattle ranch near to a hundred miles west of Falls City, outside of Fairbury. Evie had been right in assuming Jack had saved a lot of money. He had not only enough to buy the ranch, but to keep the both of them living comfortably there for several years, even if the ranch never turned a dime.

Jack knew cattle, though, and had told her that he'd do just fine with the ranch. She'd watched him negotiate the purchase with the owner, who had been passing through town on the way to St. Joseph, Missouri to look for a buyer for the property, and she had been extremely impressed. He not only knew cattle, he knew the business.

Evie reminded herself that he had owned a cattle ranch years before. She was excited beyond all reason to see him do so again. She couldn't wait to see him on the ranch, working with the cattle and the land, coming home to her each evening. It was everything she had wanted in the back of her mind but never thought she'd have, and the anticipation of it filled her with a joy she'd never known.

Despite their circumstances, they had managed to save each other. His friend Thomas had told her privately how much he believed that meeting her had been an outright miracle. He'd told her that he had nearly become convinced that nothing would save Jack from the road he'd let himself fall upon. Reverend Jarrett had proudly declared that he'd never been more pleased to be wrong.

As she left the saloon, she saw her husband standing beside the horses, Patriot and Applejack. She smiled again as she thought of the name. It never failed to touch her how sweet and charming Jack could be. When he wanted to be.

Reaching out a hand to help her mount, he gave her a warm smile.

"You ready, Mrs. Hannity?"

"Evie," she corrected with a playful grin.

"We're not that friendly," he replied, mirroring her grin.

She leaned down, and he reached up to gently kiss her lips, the tenderness of the gesture saying all they ever needed to hear.

As she looked into his eyes, she remembered the morning after they'd been married, waking slowly, curled up in his warm, safe embrace. Soon, they'd be in their own bed, on their own land, waking up that way every single day. There was no closer image of heaven.

With that, thoughts of his late wife entered her mind. Lucy had once had everything she was about to, and it had been taken from all of them. Evie vowed to never take a single instant for granted, and would love him with all she had, every second she had with him, be it one year or a hundred. Her heart ached for the woman who had everything, including her life taken from her so brutally, and for the man she had left behind.

Evie turned her eyes to the clear, blue sky and sent out a message of thanks for the wonderful woman Jack had loved, who had taught him how to love. Evie may have brought that back in him, but it was Lucy who had first captured his heart.

What life would bring them, nobody could predict, but they would face it together. The joys, the sorrows, the struggles, they would face it all together. As long as she had Jack, she'd be just fine.

Jack had saved her, no doubt about it, in more ways than one. Her own personal Saint.

As Jack mounted Patriot beside her, he wiped his brow, settled his hat comfortably back on his head and turned to regard her a long moment before he smiled softly and spoke.

"Let's go home."

www.ingramcontent.com/pod-product-compliance
Lightning Source LLC
Chambersburg PA
CBHW071747190726
48292CB00003B/902